D1799845

THE NINE LIVES OF

JACOB FALLADA

NEIL RANDALL

j.new books

jinhae/royersford

j.new books

This is a work of fiction. Names, characters, places, and incidents are a product of the author's imagination. Locales and public names are sometimes used for atmospheric purposes. Any resemblance to actual people, living or dead, or to businesses, companies, events, institutions, or locales is completely coincidental.

The Nine Lives of Jacob Fallada Copyright © 2019 by Neil Randall

All rights reserved. Printed in the United States of America. No part of this publication may be reproduced, distributed or transmitted in any form or by any means, including photocopying, recording, or other electronic or mechanical methods, without the prior written permission of the publisher, except in the case of brief quotations embodied in critical reviews and certain other noncommercial uses permitted by copyright law. For permission requests, write to the publisher, addressed "Attention: Permissions Coordinator," J New Books 105 110 Dreamville, Jinhae Gu, Changwon-si 51701 Republic of Korea or email permissions@jnewbooks

Cover Design by Liana Moisescu

ISBN-978-1-7339388-1-5

This book is dedicated to the surgeons at King's Lynn's Queen Elizabeth Hospital who performed two life-saving stomach operations on me in March of this year, and the consultants, doctors, nurses, medical staff and ambulance crew, without whom I would never have seen this book published.

1

The Tranquillity of Solitude

J acob Fallada couldn't work out what the older boys were doing, why they were gathering so many boulders from the beach and stacking them in front of a rock pool. But every time he asked them, he was either ignored completely or told to mind his own business, and he had to amuse himself with a plastic bucket and spade, building sandcastles which quickly disintegrated into a crumbly nothingness.

Disappointed, a little bored, Jacob glanced over his shoulder at his aunt, asleep in a deckchair, face reddened by the sun, snoring steadily, a dog-eared romance novel balanced precariously on her knees. Ever since they arrived this morning, she had continually shooed him away. 'Go and play down there, with the other children'. It had been the same every single day of the summer holidays so far. And her indifference towards him, her impatience, how she could barely stand his company for more than two minutes without complaining, made him increasingly anxious to make friends.

Plucking up the courage, he approached one of the older boys again.

"Can I help? Can I come and play over here? Promise I won't get in the way."

Only to receive the sternest, nastiest rebuff yet.

"Piss off out of it, you little bastard." And a shove in the chest for his trouble. "We're not wasting our time babysitting a brat like you, running around in your dirty old underpants."

It wasn't so much the harshness of his words (Jacob had heard much worse from his aunt), or the shove that almost knocked him off his feet, or the jibe about the bikini briefs he wore in place of standard swimming trunks, but the way this boy's face creased, displaying a level of irritation, disdain, hatred almost, that really took Jacob aback.

Lowering his head, he trudged back over to his bucket and spade. But after building a few more derisory sandcastles, he was just as disappointed and bored as before and decided to mimic the older boys' actions. Unseen at first, he too started to collect stones from the top end of the beach and gather them at the edge of a nearby rock pool. As he did so, he was able to scrutinise their pool at much closer quarters, and finally worked out exactly what they had been doing. Now the tide was coming in, they were diverting the rising water levels, channelling it from the sea, ensuring a steady onrush of water into their pool at all times. This ingenious yet simple provision fascinated Jacob, and he was determined to use the same technique to construct his own personal pool for the remainder of the day, or at least until the tide came all the way in.

So absorbed did he become in his new copycat activities, he didn't realise that his movements had finally come to the notice of the other boys. As he started to construct a channel of stones to divert the rising water, three of the biggest, burliest amongst the group made a blindside dash for him, knocking over all the stones he had just painstakingly stacked.

"Ha! That'll teach you. You'll never build a pool as good as ours."

Undeterred, Jacob began to rescue the toppled stones from the rock pool and reconstruct the channel, only for the same triumvirate to repeat their blindside dash of a few minutes ago, knocking each stone back into the water.

Sensing the futility of the exercise, that no matter how many times he attempted to reconstruct the channel, the boys would never tire of rushing over and knocking the stones into the water, Jacob gave up altogether. Even if he played quietly on his own, he thought to himself, some distance from the others, they still wouldn't accept his presence. And it was this sense of realisation, of injustice that compelled Jacob Fallada to do something that would have grave ramifications for the rest of his life.

Picking up a weighty stone, Jacob walked over to the boys now dive-bombing into their ever-deepening pool, splashing around, laughing and jostling with each other. Slowly but with purpose, he drew his arm back and threw the stone into the middle of the group. As soon as Jacob let go, he knew the stone's final (and perhaps intended) destination—that it was going to hit the boy who had been so rude and abrupt to him earlier. Still, the moment of impact seemed to take an eternity. It was as if Jacob could see the projectile arc and dip through the air. For many years, he was haunted by the familiar seaside sensations which became amplified in the moments between throwing the stone and it meeting its target, the collection of sounds, smells, a kind of nostalgia in reverse, how all the things which defined his summer holidays were encapsulated in that one single moment: childish voices, high-pitched laughter, the sound of waves softly breaking on the shore, the grainy feel of sand in between his toes

Then the stone crashed into the side of the boy's head with a sickening-sounding thud.

Screaming, he fell to the wet sand. And there was another moment, just as condensed and stretched out of shape, where nobody in the immediate vicinity quite knew what had happened, or who (more importantly) had been responsible. Then time started to move at normal speed again, and Jacob stared at the stricken boy howling and writhing around on the sand, he looked at the ugly gash to his forehead leaking dark blood, at the thick stringy spittle hanging from his lips as he cried, like strands of melted cheese, and something very odd, yet very neat and symmetrical registered with him. For the agonised look on the boy's face mirrored the angry look of earlier—they were on the same spectrum of extreme emotion—and it seemed apt somehow that, in the space of a very short period of time, Jacob had been responsible for the manifestation of both those expressions.

Eventually (although in real time only a minute or two had elapsed), the boy's mother rushed over from the top end of the beach. With soft, practised words of reassurance, she calmed her son down and helped him up into a sitting position, shushing him and telling him not to cry.

"It's okay, it's okay," she repeated. "You're going to be just fine."

A minute or two after that, a member of the Saint John's

ambulance crew, a squat man with a sizeable paunch and great sweat patches under his arms, arrived on the scene. Crouching, he took the now sniffing and sobbing boy's chin in his hand and tilted his head to the side.

"Cor, that's a nasty bang to the head you've had there, son. But don't you worry, you'll live."

In the aftermath of the incident, as this man cleaned and dressed the boy's wound, not one adult (or child, for that matter) asked who had thrown the stone. There were no re-criminations whatsoever; the whole thing had been passed off as an accident, boys in high spirits rushing around, throwing stones into rock pools. And Jacob trudged back over to his aunt, who had, by this time, woken from her slumber.

As soon as he reached her deckchair, she lunged forward and grabbed his wrist.

"I saw you," she hissed into his ear. "I saw you throw that stone, I saw you hit that poor lad on the head."

Her outburst was so unexpected that Jacob found himself breaking out in tears, pleading with her to forgive him, saying that it was just an accident, and if only the boys had let him join in with their game then none of this would have happened.

"Think very carefully about what you've done today, young man. I've got a good mind to march you straight back over there and report you to the police. You could've killed someone, throwing great big rocks around, willy-nilly."

"I'm sorry, I didn't mean to do it. I promise I'll never throw stones again."

Such was the level of his upset, the choking nature of those tears, his aunt had no other option than to pack up their things and take him home.

Once indoors, Jacob started to feel incredibly guilty and

ashamed. He couldn't believe that he had acted with such violent calculation, because he knew that he had fully intended to march over to the rock pool and throw that stone at that particular boy. In painful clarity, he replayed the whole incident over in his head; he could see the stone travelling through the air, could hear that horrible thud when it smacked into the boy's skull, could clearly visualise all that blood seeping into the wet sand, could feel that awful churning feeling of regret in the pit of his stomach—that desperate need to turn back time.

These remembered visions disturbed Jacob so much, he ran upstairs to his bedroom, took out his drawing book and colouring pencils and began to sketch out the scene, began to draw with a concentration and skill that he had never drawn with before.

Hours passed.

That evening, Jacob had been scheduled to attend a birthday party. The lofty manner in which his aunt had presented news of the invitation told him that, despite his own reservations about going, it was a great honour.

"I had to practically get down on bended knee to convince Harold's mother to invite you along."

For obvious reasons, Jacob assumed that he would no longer be allowed to go, that his actions at the beach were worthy of some prolonged form of punishment, that there was no way his aunt would simply forget the matter. But that didn't prove to be the case.

"Not that you deserve to go to any party," she said, with real bitterness in her voice, "not that you deserve any jelly and ice cream, or birthday cake, but I've made plans for this evening, so I've got no choice."

Due to their straitened finances, Jacob could only give Harold, a slightly older boy he had barely ever spoken to before, the most modest of presents: a handkerchief set left over from Christmas. In comparison, the other children with their smart clean clothes, shoes new and shiny, had purchased elaborate gifts for their genuine, actual friend, gifts which were gratefully received.

"Erm, thanks, Jacob," Harold had said under the watchful eye of his mother. "A hankie. How thoughtful."

For the rest of the evening, Jacob spent much of his time on his own, standing in a corner, sipping cherryade and nibbling on shop-bought sausage rolls, looking on as the other children laughed and joked around, danced, kicked balloons high into the air. Not that he courted company. Still his mind was occupied by the incident at the beach. Still he was racked with guilt, haunted by visions of the boy he had so discriminately injured. Only when it was time for parlour games like Pass the Parcel and Simon Says did he participate, interact, endure all the casual but expected humiliations. For, every time the parcel was supposed to be handed to Jacob, the boy sitting next to him would craftily bypass him, tossing the present to the boy seated in the next chair along. And whenever someone called out Simon Says, one of the children would invariably shout something like 'Kick Jacob up the backside'.

Later, they assembled in the sun-drenched back garden. Of all the gifts the birthday boy had received, the set of junior golf clubs from his father had clearly given him the most pleasure. Keen to show it off to his friends (and Jacob), Harold marched them all outside, sunk a tee into the lush green grass, placed a ball on top of it and showcased his swing, demonstrating exactly how to hit a golf ball, and inviting them all to have a try afterwards. With no little skill for boys their age, they chipped a series of balls up towards an improvised pin: a stripy umbrella turned upside down and wedged into the ground just like the tee. Having no interest in sports of any kind, Jacob dreaded his turn. Already the day had been traumatic enough without him making a fool out of himself with a thin, flimsy implement that looked wholly unsuited to hitting a ball of such relatively small size.

"Go on, Fallada," said one of the boys, handing Jacob the golf club. "You're up next."

Before he had even addressed the ball, it was clear, just by the baffled and uncertain way in which Jacob wielded the club, that he wasn't possessed of much coordination or natural sporting ability. That was undoubtedly why the birthday boy, perhaps bitter at having to invite Jacob in the first place, decided to play a prank on him, a prank that was to go swiftly and spectacularly wrong. Whether Harold was ignorant of golfing etiquette, or not possessed of the basic common sense that tells a person to never walk behind a player about to draw the club back and strike a ball, or whether he merely doubted that Jacob had the gumption to lift the club and take any shot whatsoever, he crept up behind him meaning to tug his dated, ill-fitting trousers down from the waist and was dealt such a resounding blow to the skull, he was sent stumbling backwards, collapsing to the ground.

Jacob wheeled around in horror. Like that moment on the beach, he saw another boy writhing and screaming in agony, with a great big gash to the forehead.

"Mrs James, Mrs James," the children started to call for Harold's mother.

Almost immediately, she rushed out of the back door.

"My word! Whatever has happened?"

Kneeling before her son, she whispered the same soft, practised words of reassurance that Jacob had heard at the beach earlier, helped him up into a sitting position, and assessed the injury.

"Shush, don't worry, darling. You've taken a nasty bang to the head, but you'll be just fine."

Much to Jacob's bewilderment, and despite the fact that Mrs James was busy stemming the flow of blood with a wet cloth, all the other children present in the garden at the time of the incident attested to his guilt, that he had known that Harold was behind him and had deliberately struck him a blow with the golf club.

"Don't be so silly," she said. "This was clearly an accident. You should never walk behind someone with a golf club in their hands. If Harry wants to take up the game properly in the future, he's learnt a painful but valuable lesson today."

And despite the vociferous protests to the contrary, she remained steadfast in her view.

"But, erm…" she said to Jacob once the wound had been dressed and they had reconvened indoors, "perhaps it might be best if we called your aunt to pick you up now, eh?"

***

"I just don't know what I'm going to do with you," she complained on their return home. "All I wanted was a nice relaxing evening with friends, and I have to come and pick you up early because you've attacked another boy."

"I didn't attack him," Jacob contended, struggling to control his trembling bottom lip. "It was an accident. He walked behind me as I was about to hit a golf ball, something Mrs James said you should never do."

"Two accidents in one day! I don't think so. Now, get to your room. I'm sick of the sight of you, I really am."

That night, Jacob found it difficult to sleep. In the silent darkness, he questioned the nature of his own actions. For, had the striking of the second blow really been an accident?

Had he not spotted Harold creeping up on him out of the corner of his eye? Had he not heard the other boys whispering and giggling behind his back? Had he not wanted to avenge the painful and unnecessary teasing he had endured all evening? Put simply, in a very childlike, counter-intuitive manner, Jacob questioned his own personality, whether he was a good or bad boy, someone capable of inflicting pain on others. And the fact that he couldn't reconcile what had happened today with his own shifting sense of self made him very worried indeed.

In the days that followed, Jacob spent all his time alone drawing in his bedroom, emerging only to eat the meagre fare—beans on toast, corned beef hash, bread-and-pullet—which constituted meals under his aunt's roof. In striking detail, and with the same concentration and skill as before, he started to reimagine both incidents on paper, to draw the beach, the older boys, the rock pools, then the party scene, the children dancing around a front room decorated with balloons and ribbons. He then proceeded to sketch out the unpleasant aspects of that long, testing day: the older boy's horrible twisted facial expression when he shoved him in the chest, the same boy lying sprawled out on the wet sand, crying in pain, how the blood poured from the deep cut to his forehead, how his mother cradled him in her arms like a baby; he even drew a picture of his aunt when she unexpectedly grabbed his wrist and hissed into his ear, telling him that she had witnessed everything.

Moving swiftly on, he then drew pictures of the party, how the two boys sitting either side of him when they were playing Pass the Parcel made sure that he never got his hands on the present, the object of the game, and the way they laughed behind his back when they played Simon Says. Next, he drew a series of pictures set in the back garden, pictures of Harold creeping up behind him, the moment the golf club collided with his head, the agonised look on his face as he writhed around on the grass, and the way Mrs James crouched before him and dabbed the wound with a cloth.

Finally, he drew pictures of the kinds of people he would like to know, friends he had never had the good fortune to make, adults who treated him with warmth and kindness, giving them certain characteristics he particularly admired, like wide smiles or jaunty gaits, long flowing hair and colourful clothes, compiling a whole assortment of likeable imaginary friends and family members: Robert, Jennifer, Jermaine, and Jackie. Or: Auntie Pansy, Doctor Shepherdson, Mum and Dad #2.

Fully absorbed in his artwork, in trying to recapture scenes that had so unsettled him, scenes in which he hadn't perhaps acted in the best possible way, he filled drawing book after drawing book. He came to enjoy the long, swelteringly hot days indoors, the sense of enclosure, the tranquillity of solitude, of being firmly and safely ensconced in his own private hideaway, far from other people and all the nasty things they could say and do to him.

On odd occasions, his aunt would hammer on his bedroom door and tell him to turn off the light, that electricity cost a fortune these days and that she couldn't afford to have him burning a lamp till the early hours of each morning.

On other occasions, he would hear her talking to neighbours over the fence in the back garden. 'I don't know what's wrong with the boy. Only took him in out of the goodness of my heart. But, ever since I've been lumbered with him, he's been nothing but trouble. Now he just sits in his room all day drawing in his colouring books'. And: 'He's due back at school soon and hasn't left the house for three weeks. Expect I'll have to get the GP or one of the teachers out to see him.'

One Thursday in early September, Jacob's aunt called him down from his bedroom.

"Jacob," she said as he walked into the kitchen. "This is Mr Preston."

Jacob stared confusedly at the neat, smartly dressed, middle-aged man sitting across from his aunt, a cup of tea in his hand.

"You remember Mr Preston from school, don't you?"

Jacob half nodded his head. While not old enough to be in any of Mr Preston's classes, he nonetheless distinctly remembered seeing him on numerous occasions, foremost during morning assembly.

"Well, as you're due to be starting school again soon, Mr Preston thought he'd come out and have a quick chat with you, about all the new things you'll be doing next term."

Mr Preston put his cup down on the table.

"It's my aim to encourage all my students' academic, artistic and sporting abilities, Jacob. And your aunt has been telling me how much time you've spent drawing this summer." He flashed a warm, reassuring smile. "I'd love to see some of your pictures, if you don't mind showing them to me, that is?"

Very politely, Jacob told the teacher that he'd be happy to let him see his drawings, even though he wasn't sure if they were any good or not.

"Oh, I'm sure you're just being modest." The teacher smiled again and got to his feet. "Shall we go up to your room and have a look?"

Jacob nodded and led the way upstairs.

Once inside the bedroom, Jacob noticed the uncertain, disapproving way in which Mr Preston's darting eyes took in the sparse, impoverished space, the drab, colourless walls, metal-framed bed with a stained mattress, no under sheets or pillow case on the solitary pillow, the filthy rug that covered the bare dusty floorboards.

"My pictures are under here." Jacob dropped to his knees, reached out a hand and pulled a great big pile of drawing books out from under the bed. "Here." He stood, straightened, and handed the top one to Mr Preston.

Although clearly reluctant to sit on the bed, the teacher nonetheless hitched up his trousers so as not to crease them and perched on the furthest-most extremity of the mattress, taking the vast majority of his weight on his legs.

"And these are your pictures, Jacob, the pictures you've drawn?"

Jacob nodded and looked on as the teacher opened the first book and flicked through the pages, looked on as a grave, puzzled, maybe even disturbed expression broke out across his face.

"These are, erm…very strange, mature, sophisticated pictures, Jacob," he said, putting the sketchbook aside and getting to his feet. "If you want my advice, don't show them to anyone else until you understand what they really mean."

2

...and Punishment

Jacob Fallada trudged across a muddy playing-field. Shivering, attired in only a rugby shirt, a pair of shorts, ankle socks, and plimsolls, he felt each icy gust of wind like a brutal lash from a horsewhip. No matter how hard he'd tried to convince the sports master of his unfitness to participate this morning—his terrible cough, a sprained ankle, an in-growing toenail—he was ordered to change into his P.E. kit and join the other children outside.

"But, sir, I'm not really cut out for sports in general, and really do feel as if my time would be better spent in the art room perfecting my—"

"Cross-country running, Fallada," said Mr Breeze-Hampton, a stern disciplinarian, ex-armed forces, veteran marathon runner, triathlete, general man of steel. "You don't want to miss out, boy. Six miles. Invigorating in this weather, what? Now, go on, get out there. Breathe in the cold, crisp air. You'll soon warm up once you're in stride."

Buffeted by the elements, Jacob struggled over towards the start line, where the other pupils were either limbering up—stretching, touching their toes, rolling their necks—or huddling close together, near bare spindly hedgerows, trying to shelter from the wind.

Like the first circle of his own personal hell, Jacob knew exactly what awaited him, he knew he would quickly fall behind the main pack of runners, be lapped time and again, slip over on innumerable occasions, scrape his knees and elbows, get drenched to the bone; he knew he would be bundled into the woods by the older, bigger boys, be pummelled and kicked, maybe even stripped naked. He knew the cruel unpleasantness of each likely humiliation before he had even a chance to contemplate the serial indignity of the showers.

"Get off me!" a girlish voice pleaded and died on the blustery wind.

Jacob looked right and left, but not one of his fellow pupils seemed to have heard what he had just heard—they continued to limber up or shelter just like they had before.

Confused, Jacob looked right and left again, surveying the gloomy playing-field and surrounding woodland. But in the sweeping rain that had just started to fall, he couldn't see anything out of the ordinary. Only when a second muffled cry broke out did he realise exactly where it was coming from—behind him.

He turned to see three bigger, older boys—the usual suspects—crowding around Michela Murphy, shouting and jeering, jostling her closer to a deep drainage ditch that always oozed thick dark mud this time of year. This confused Jacob all over again. Michela was one of the nicest, prettiest, most popular girls in his year, one of the few people who gave him the time of day, who said hello if they happened to pass, who occasionally engaged him in conversation, who treated him with consideration, not contempt. Why would she be alone with notorious bullies of the most reprehensible kind?

Keen to find out, to perhaps come to her aid, Jacob made his way over to the ditch. Only for something completely contrary to happen.

For, no sooner had he reached them than the boys picked Michela up, roughly grabbing her by the wrists and ankles.

"Best we teach this one a lesson," said Shane Pearson, the biggest and bulkiest of the three. "Always walking 'round with your nose in the air, thinking you're better than everyone else."

"Yeah," said Zac Greene. "A dunking in that ditch is sure to do the trick."

In the ensuing melee, as the teenage girl shouted and screamed and kicked out her legs, the third boy, Will Storey, lost his grip of her ankles. As he went flailing down to one knee, his eyes met Jacob's.

"You, piss-pants Fallada, grab her other ankle. Now! We haven't got much time."

"What? No. I—"

"Do it, Fallada!" shouted Greene, clasping hold of one of Michela's wrists. "And we might just leave you alone come shower time."

Before he really knew what he was doing, Jacob was actually assisting the bullies, grabbing Michela's other ankle and helping them manoeuvre her closer to the ditch.

"Right," said Storey. "A one, a two, a one, two, three, four."

At first, it was as if they only meant to scare her, to swing her back and forth, time and again, pausing for a fraction of a second, as if they truly meant to let go, only to draw her back in again at the last moment. But something happened on the fifth or sixth dummy run, where each boy, Jacob included, let go of a wrist or ankle at one and the same time, tossing the girl high into the air, propelling her upwards with tremendous force, only to come splashing down in the ditch with a squelchy sounding plop.

There was a moment of total silence, where even the swirling elements seemed to have been emphatically quieted. They stared at Michela, wedged head first in the ditch.

"Shit. Quick, lads, let's get out of here."

The three bigger, older boys sprinted into the woods, quickly disappearing into the undergrowth. The rain continued to hammer down. Wind whistled through the naked tree branches. Jacob had no idea what to do.

"Fallada," shouted Breeze-Hampton. "What the hell's going on over there?"

He didn't respond; he just stood rooted to the spot as the sports master and two of his colleagues rushed over.

"My God!" cried Breeze-Hampton. "That's Michela Murphy. How on earth did she…? Quick. Let's get her out of there. She might drown."

By this time, as the three teachers attempted to remove Michela from the ditch, all the other children had made their way over, to find out what exactly what was going on.

"Is she dead?"

"I can see her knickers."

"Who'd do such a thing?"

"Someone's going to be in big, big trouble."

"Wouldn't surprise me if the police got involved."

"I do hope she's all right."

In the direct aftermath, where Michela's welfare was of paramount importance, after the teachers had carefully removed her from the ditch and laid her out on the grass, covering her with thick woollen blankets, when the ambulance crew dashed across the playing-field, knelt beside her, assessing her injuries, when they fastened a brace to her neck and lifted her up onto a stretcher, when they carried her to the ambulance, securing her in the back, when the ambulance itself had sped off in a wail of sirens and flashing blue lights, there were no real recriminations, no inquest as to what had happened and who had been responsible. Stony-faced, Breeze-Hampton told everyone to go and get showered and changed.

"After this most unedifying event, I know your thoughts and prayers will be with Michela."

That afternoon, talk of the incident dominated the school corridors. In the canteen at lunch-time, Jacob heard more rabid speculation as to the identity of the culprits and the ultimate punishment they deserved. More worryingly, wild rumours abounded regarding Michela's condition.

"Paralysed from the waist down"…"broke her neck"… "never walk again" was the general and bleak prognosis.

All of which made Jacob feel terribly guilty. In English class, he couldn't concentrate on the final few chapters of Great Expectations, even though he considered it to be one of the finest books he had ever read. Dark forebodings clouded his mind. He knew there was no way he would escape punishment for his part in the incident. Not just because he had indeed been involved, but because unfortunates like him, people who never stood up for themselves, always ended up taking the blame.

It was almost inevitable, therefore, when the headmaster, a tall, rangy, pseudo-educationalist with a chicken-like neck, tapped lightly on the classroom door.

"Sorry to interrupt, Niall," he said to the English teacher. "But I want to have a word with one of your pupils."

He squinted up his deep-set, bespectacled eyes and surveyed the room.

"Fallada, Jacob Fallada. I need you to come with me, boy."

In silence, he followed the headteacher down the corridor towards his office, dreading what awaited him.

"You're in a lot of trouble," he said, when they reached the reception area. "Before she was rushed into theatre, Michela told her parents all about the incident. In their magnanimity, however, they have decided not to report the matter to the police. But, as their daughter recuperates following emergency surgery, they wanted to talk to you face-to-face, before heading back up to the hospital."

"Talk to me?"

"That's correct."

They walked into his neat yet musty-smelling office. Seated in visitors' chairs, with their backs to the door, were Mr and Mrs Murphy. Jacob had seen them many times before, at certain school events—fetes, plays, fundraisers, sports days. They always struck him as an idealised vision of parental perfection. Much younger than the other mums and dads, they were relaxed, trendy, chatty, always smiling and holding hands. They appeared to like being around each other, which wasn't the case with the vast majority of sniping, begrudging adults Jacob had observed in his fourteen and a half years so far.

"Sit down, Jacob." The headteacher directed him to a plastic-backed chair in the far corner, his own personal if somewhat diminished dock.

Mr and Mrs Murphy followed him with their eyes as he walked across the room and took a seat. As he shifted position—a more self-conscious than truly necessary adjustment—he stole a glimpse at them out of the corner of his eye. Both looked tired and drawn, more than angry or upset

"Michela has told us everything," said Mr Murphy. "She

told us that you threw her headfirst into that ditch."

Jacob didn't know what to say, if he should refute the charges made against him, argue, plead his innocence, point out various undeniable logistical facts involved—that it was impossible for a boy of his size to have thrown Michela into the ditch alone. But if he did so, he would, undoubtedly, have to name the true culprits, and that would lead to unpleasant repercussions, so he said nothing.

"Now," Mr Murphy went on, "we know children don't like to tell tales on others, to get their friends in trouble, so we're not going to sit here and conduct an excruciating kangaroo court. No. What we want you to do, Jacob, is not only apologise for what you have done today, but to also make amends."

"Amends?" Jacob repeated, as if he had no understanding of what the word meant.

"That's correct," said Mrs Murphy. "As you no doubt appreciate, we're furious about what has happened to Michela. She's a kind, caring girl who never has a bad word to say about anyone. But due to our philosophical beliefs, we've never agreed with any form of retribution, revenge, an eye for an eye. We feel such concepts are retarded, self-defeating in many respects. But we do believe that people, youngsters especially, should be held responsible for their actions, that they should attempt to make up for any wrongdoing. For that reason, we would like you to help Michela during her long road to recovery."

"Long road? Is…Is she going to be all right?"

Husband and wife shared a quick, anxious look.

"At this stage, it's hard to say," said Mr Murphy. "Until the swelling goes down, the doctors won't know the full extent of her spinal injuries or whether she'll make a full recovery or not."

"She…She might be paralysed, you mean?"

Mrs Murphy squeezed her eyes shut, as if to halt the tears that threatened to stream down her cheeks.

"Let's hope and pray it doesn't come to that," said Mr Murphy. "But, as and when Michela returns home, we want you to call round each day and sit with her, keep her company, entertain her in any way she so wishes. We want you to make up for the horrible deed you perpetrated."

Two weeks later, when Michela was indeed discharged from the hospital, Jacob was called to the headmaster's office again.

"Right, Fallada, Mr and Mrs Murphy would like you to make good on your pledge to them. They want you to call round to their house this afternoon and sit with Michela. Don't worry. I've contacted your aunt. She knows exactly where you are, and how long you are required to be there."

After school, Jacob walked the short distance to the Murphy home. In the past, he had often admired the house on his way to school. A vast, new, red-bricked property, with high windows, a sweeping garden to the rear, a neat shingled drive out front bordered by colourful flowerbeds, and a basketball hoop above a double-garage, it looked so different from his own house: a council property, with damp up the walls, no central heating, or carpets on the upstairs landing, a dwelling, a tatty domicile more than a real, warm, welcoming home.

Stern-faced, Mr and Mrs Murphy were waiting on the front doorstep.

"Right on time," said Michela's father, tapping his wristwatch. "Now, as you've probably been made aware, Michela's surgery was a great success. While not one hundred per cent guaranteed, the doctors are extremely confident of her making a full recovery. However, over the next few weeks, bed rest, recuperation is of paramount importance. That's where you come in, Jacob. Being cooped up all day, young people, used to running around with their friends, can go a little stir crazy. It's your job, therefore, to help Michela through this most trying period."

They led Jacob into the house, politely asked him to remove his shoes, then pointed him in the direction of Michela's bedroom.

"It's the second door on the left," said Mrs Murphy. "You can't miss it—there's a big Michela's Room sign on the door." She gave his shoulder a firm, encouraging pat. "Up you go. We'll be along shortly to speak to you both."

Jacob climbed the stairs, knocked on the door, identified himself and waited.

"Come in," said Michela.

He turned the handle and walked inside the room.

Immediately, he was struck by what an incredibly neat, ordered, and well-appointed space this was, full of everything a teenager could possibly require: a desk and chair, writing materials, pencils, papers, a crammed bookcase, transistor radio. On the walls were all of Michela's various awards, framed certificates, a shelf above the desk housed her many sporting trophies, over thirty shiny golden statuettes, for swimming, tennis, chess, netball.

"Hello, Jacob," she said, blank-faced. "Please, take a seat."

A wicker chair had been set out beside the bed.

"Thank you."

They sat in silence for a full minute, maybe more. Jacob could barely look at her. Not just because of the protective cast encasing her whole upper body, but because there was something missing, the usual bright smile, as if she had been robbed of the vitality that had once defined her, that was so infectious and endearing, as if those three bullies had stolen it when they assaulted her that day.

Michela was first to speak again.

"I suppose you're wondering why I told everyone that it was you who threw me into that ditch?"

Jacob half lifted his head and nodded.

"Well, I was pretty shaken up by the incident. I couldn't believe that you were involved. I mean, what have I ever done to you? I'm one of the few people in the entire school who's civil to you. It really hurt my feelings. And for that reason, I wanted revenge. I wanted to make you feel as bad as I felt when you helped those horrible boys. For the next three weeks, therefore, I want you to be my dog."

"You...You want me to be what?"

"My dog," she repeated. "For starters, I want you to get down on all fours and sniff around the floor, like you've picked up an interesting scent."

"Erm..." Unsure if he should comply, if he had any option—if his debt of guilt was such, Michela had every right to humiliate him in this manner—Jacob nevertheless found himself dropping down on all fours and, nose to the thick carpet, sniffing around, darting this way and that, as if he had indeed picked up an interesting scent.

"That's it," she said. "Now I want you to crawl into the centre of the room and roll over onto your back."

Jacob did as instructed, rolling onto his back with his arms and legs raised in the air.

"That's a good doggy-woggy," she said in irritating baby talk. "Now, roll back onto your front, crawl over to the wardrobe, cock your leg and pretend to urinate."

While hesitant, sensing that she may well be going too far with this, he was in role now, and scampered over to the wardrobe.

"You naughty boy!" she snapped at him as soon as he

raised his leg. "If Mummy could get out of bed, she'd rub your nose in that. What a horrible, dirty dog you are."

So harsh were her words, he felt like turning around and putting things into the proper context, stating that it was her suggestion. But before he could, the door swung open and in walked Mr and Mrs Murphy.

"Ah, excellent," said Mr Murphy. "I see you've already familiarised Jacob with his new role around the house."

"New role?" said Jacob, making as to get to his feet.

"Down you dirty dog." Mrs Murphy lunged forward, past her husband. "Unruly beasts like you need discipline. Down, I say!"

Shocked, Jacob cowered and raised both hands, as if to defend himself against an incoming blow.

"Miranda is right," said Mr Murphy, gesturing for his wife to step down. "After everything that's happened, it's imperative that you undergo extensive social reprogramming. So, let's sit down, the four of us, and discuss exactly what's required of you."

Mr Murphy took the wicker chair, his wife the bed beside her daughter. Thinking nothing of it, Jacob headed straight for the opposite end of the bed, as if to perch himself on the very edge of the mattress.

"No, Jacob," said Mr Murphy, frowning. "I mean sit, really sit."

"Oh, right, yes, of course, sorry."

Vacating a position he had barely assumed, Jacob took a step away from the bed, crouched, and sat cross-legged on the floor.

"No!" Mr Murphy exploded with anger. "Sit, sit like a dog, for pity's sake!"

Shaken by the outburst, especially from someone he had always considered laid-back, mild-mannered, Jacob did exactly as he was told, sitting on the floor like a devoted dog looking up at its master.

"That's better. Now let me explain how all of this is going to work." Mr Murphy paused for a moment before continuing. "As we mentioned in the headmaster's office, we're very modern, forward-thinking parents, unshackled by any religious belief system. We are guided solely by scientific certainty, and feel, therefore, that a period of role-playing servitude would be of great benefit to the development of your character."

From his position of canine subservience, Jacob looked on, blinking his eyes in confusion, having little or no idea where any of this was headed.

"Until such a time as Michela is able to return to school, you will play the role of her devoted dog. You are, therefore, prohibited from speaking—canines cannot speak, so neither shall you. If you need to communicate with any member of the family you will bark, politely. Growling, snapping, snarling is not permitted. Neither will you be able to walk upon two legs. Most importantly, though, you must obey Michela's commands, and that of any family member, at all times. If not, we will have to resort to certain punitive measures?"

Jacob didn't like the sound of that.

"Punitive measures?"

"Silence, dog!" Once again, Mrs Murphy lunged forward, only this time she clouted Jacob around the side of the head.

"Ah!"

"Perhaps a whimper would best from now on, Jacob," said Mr Murphy, in all seriousness. "For our experiment, which we will record, type up, and present to the relevant government agency, is now well and truly underway. In regard to the punitive measures mentioned, we will start off with a little water aversion therapy. Put simply: if you fail to comply with any request or command you will have a glass of water thrown into your face." He angled his head over his shoulder. "Darling, if you'd like to fill a glass from the pitcher beside the bed."

Mrs Murphy duly got to her feet, filled a glass and handed it to her husband.

"Jacob!" he suddenly shouted. "Roll over onto your back, bark, wag your tail, lift your paw and shake my hand." Commands issued at such a rapid, gabbled rate, Jacob had no chance of complying. "Too slow." And Mr Murphy tossed a whole glass of water into his face

"Hey!" cried Jacob, shaking his sodden head.

As if anticipating such a reaction, Mrs Murphy tossed a second glass of water directly into his face.

Shocked silence.

"I think you get the idea now, don't you, Jacob?" Mr Murphy didn't wait for any show of understanding. "In your time with us, your duties will be manifold. Thrice-daily, you will bring Michela her main meals up from the kitchen. In addition, you will fetch any necessary medicine, snacks and the like from downstairs. This will, of course, necessitate certain items of apparel."

Blindly, he lifted a hand, and Mrs Murphy passed him the aforementioned apparel, item by item.

"Firstly, we have your collar and leash." He held both up for perusal and then rested them on his lap. "The former will be worn at all times, the latter only during exercise periods or whenever you need to relieve yourself in the back garden. Secondly,"—again, he blindly raised a hand, and again, Mrs Murphy handed him an item—"we have what I like to call the howdah, a customised saddle to wear upon your back with leather compartments and convenient side pouches for bowls, plates, cups, cutlery et cetera. This will, of course, only be worn when performing your serving duties.

"At night, you will sleep in the dog basket provided." He pointed to the other side of the room. "As you can see, it's been fitted with a few, erm…essential modifications. Once inside, we will activate a security system. If you move suddenly or too abruptly in the night, or if you attempt to leave the basket before the permitted time, you will receive a non-fatal but nonetheless significant electric shock."

Jacob was about to speak out, to protest at such an inhumane not to mention painful provision, but memory of their recent displays of displeasure made him think better of it.

"For now"—Mr Murphy checked his wristwatch—"it's about time to serve the evening meal. If you'd be so good as to join us downstairs, Jacob, we can load you up, as it were. We don't want our patient going hungry now, do we?"

He flashed his daughter a fatherly smile and jostled Jacob out of the door with his knees.

On the landing, he fastened the collar to Jacob's neck and insisted that he walk down the stairs on all fours—a challenging task for a biped unused to such an awkward, unusual descent, a task he only just managed to undertake without a nasty, free-falling mishap.

Once in the kitchen, Mr Murphy securely fastened the howdah to Jacob's back, skipping from right to left, tugging to test its integrity.

"Didn't budge an inch." He clapped his hands— "Excellent!"—and turned to his wife. "How's dinner coming along, darling?"

"Just about to dish up."

Even from such a lowly vantage point, Jacob got a waft of the delicious aromas coming from the hob, a distinct garlicky and roasted tomato smell, the rich redolent odour of prime meat sizzling in a pan, aromas which he had rarely if ever experienced before, and then, only when passing restaurants in town during the lunch-time rush.

"Right," said Mrs Murphy. "Here we are, one wholesome, lovingly prepared meal for our special girl."

A moment later, Jacob could feel Mr Murphy deposit each bowl, plate, knife, fork and spoon into its rightful compartment in the howdah. But before he could even think about moving, let alone working out how on earth he was going to navigate his way up the stairs with his precious savoury cargo, Mrs Murphy ducked down and stared right into his face.

"And if you spill a single drop, you dirty, dirty dog," she said, "I'll do more than rub your nose in it, you hear?"

With utmost trepidation, therefore, Jacob ambled down the hallway towards the staircase. When he reached the bottom rung and looked up, the climb looked positively Himalayan, an even more terrifying prospect than his decidedly unsteady descent of a few minutes ago. But, surprisingly—perhaps more to do with the howdah's fool-proof design than Jacob's own motor skills—he made the return trip with careful, considered ease. Not once did it feel as if any of the foodstuffs or utensils lodged on his back were going to spill out.

Once Jacob had made it into the bedroom, Mr Murphy removed the steaming bowl and other receptacles and implements from each compartment and carefully placed them down on Michela's lap.

"Thank you, Daddy."

"No problem, darling. You enjoy. Got to keep your

strength up now, haven't we?" He looked down at Jacob. "Good job, doggy." He ruffled his hair. "And don't worry, we haven't forgotten about you. Look. Over there." He pointed towards a bowl on the floor by the basket. "Go on. Go and get your treat."

Eagerly, his appetite not only stimulated by the delicious kitchen smells but by the fact that it must've been five, maybe even six o'clock by now, long past his usual dinner time, he scampered over to the other side of the room, assuming his bowl would be full of the same wholesome, lovingly prepared food, that he would be treated to the same sizzling meat and whatever foodstuff had been roasted in garlic and tomato sauce. But when he poked his nose into the bowl, he was appalled to discover a pile of thick, jellified, heinous-smelling dog food, the like that sustains any domesticated hound in any household around the world.

"Cor, this is delicious," Michela said teasingly, drawing out each syllable. "How's your food, doggy-woggy? You like that slimy slop, all that condemned meat, do you?"

Both father and daughter broke out in uproarious laughter.

***

"Remember, darling, this is your time," said Mr Murphy, standing by the bedroom door. "First and foremost, Jacob is here to keep you entertained. So, have some fun with him, get him to clown around in any way you see fit. But don't lose sight of the fact that he's a dog now. If we ignore Professor Randolph's guidelines, if we're lenient on Jacob, if we treat him like a normal, kind, considerate fourteen-year-old boy—something he has proved far from being—he'll learn nothing from the exercise. Okay?" He edged out of the door, saying, "Have fun," over his shoulder.

Michela shot a glance over at Jacob.

"Right, doggy-woggy, what shall we do?" She screwed up her face. "I know. Come over here…that's it, close to the bed."

With difficulty, encumbered by the weighty body cast, she dangled her right hand over the edge of the mattress.

"Lick my hand."

Reluctant, but fully aware of the consequences of any act of disobedience or non-compliance, Jacob ducked forward, stuck out his tongue and lapped away at her palm, in the way he remembered dogs licking his own hand in the past.

"Ah! Ugh! That tickles!" She quickly withdrew her hand. "That's disgusting. The feel of your horrible wet little tongue." She made a great show of wiping her hand on the duvet cover. "Bad dog. Don't ever do that to Mummy again. She doesn't want to catch any of your nasty doggy diseases now, does she?"

They remained silent for what felt like a long period of time, from Jacob's perspective, anyway.

Then Michela said in a gentle, enquiring tone of voice, "Jacob, can I ask you something? Why are you always on your own? Why don't you have any friends at school, people you hang around with on a regular basis? I mean, everyone else, no matter how quiet or shy or not particularly sure of themselves, has got at least one good friend."

Even if Jacob had been able to respond, he would've struggled to have come up with an answer. It wasn't as if he deliberately sought solitude; he'd just never seemed to fit in anywhere, and wasn't a very outgoing character, the kind of person comfortable approaching new people. Besides, his artistic work and interests were very time-consuming.

"Come on, Jacob. You can talk now, now it's just you and me. You don't have to put on an act twenty-four hours' around the clock. You know that? We're friends, right?—

classmates."

This unexpected show of kindness, suggesting that perhaps it was Michela's parents who were the sadistic proponents of this silly game and that he may have an ally in his fellow pupil, the person he would no doubt be spending the most time with these next few weeks, made Jacob lower his guard. But no sooner had he opened his mouth in preparation to answer than Michela started to shout and scream.

"Mum, Dad, the dog, it's talking to me, it's not playing by the rules; it's ruining everything."

In a ludicrously short space of time, as if Mr Murphy had been waiting outside the door, on stand-by, should any such indiscretion take place, he dashed into the room with a small handheld taser.

"Don't say you weren't warned."

***

When Jacob came round, he lay sprawled out in the basket in the corner of the darkened bedroom. From the dim moonglow that reflected through the thin curtains, he could see Michela tucked up in bed, could see the covers shift with the soft rising and falling of each breath. Scared to move, he remained as still as possible, trying to ignore the pressure that had built up in both bowel and bladder. So desperate was he, he seriously toyed with the idea of relieving himself there and then and suffering the consequences, the shouting and violent recrimination.

It was like a godsend, therefore, when he heard voices and footsteps padding down the landing. A moment later, there was a light tapping on Michela's door and Mr Murphy walked into the room. Creeping over to the bed, he leaned close, checking to see if his daughter was still asleep. When satisfied that she was, he shuffled over to the basket, knelt and disenabled the security system. In turn, Jacob bolted upright, whimpered and rubbed his head against his leg.

"I thought so," he said, readying the lead he had to hand. "Come on you," he added, peering over Jacob's body, no doubt to check that the cushion and bedding inside the basket remained unsoiled. "Let's get you outside."

Much to his own surprise, Jacob performed his daily functions with neither embarrassment nor restraint.

"Good doggy," said Mr Murphy, ducking down with a plastic carrier bag over his hand and scooping up Jacob's recently deposited waste product. "Look at the size of this! Just what I need for my allotment."

As he stood and straightened, Jacob was shocked to see that he now wore the taser in a holster around his waist, like a Sheriff in some lawless town. With awful clarity, Jacob remembered yesterday's painful jab, the way the electrical charge pulsed through his body, the horrible singed hair smell which rose to his nostrils. To know that he was only ever moments away from another assault, set him on edge, making him painfully aware of the consequences of any perceived misbehaviour, how one word from Michela could subject him to more of the same.

"Come on, boy." Mr Murphy tugged at his lead. "You've got work to do this morning. Our little girl needs her breakfast. Big day today. She's seeing the consultant again. Fingers crossed, she might even be rid of that horrible cast."

***

"Oh, I'm so happy, Mummy." Voices roused Jacob from a fitful slumber.

Secured in the basket, he tentatively lifted his head, careful not to trip the electric shock mechanism, and tried to listen in to what was being said downstairs, but all he could hear were fragments, isolated words, fractured sentences, nothing else to indicate if Michela's visit to the consultant had been a success or a disappointment.

Only when the bedroom door swung open could he confirm what he dearly hoped. For, not only was Michela walking unaided, but the cast had been removed from her upper body.

"Don't get too excited, dog," she said, as if interpreting the hopeful look in his eyes. "I've still got to wear this stupid thing."

She pulled up her pretty peach-coloured blouse and showed him the back brace now adorning her thin girlish frame.

"And the doctors aren't sure when I'll be able to go back to school." She shot him a pouty, dismissive look. "Now, get yourself downstairs and fetch me my medication."

Dutifully, Jacob went down to the kitchen, where he found Mr and Mrs Murphy absorbed in a flurry of activities—slicing bread, assembling a salad, putting cupcakes and chocolate-chip cookies onto a serving platter. From the sheer numbers of plastic cups and paper plates they eventually loaded him up with, he could only assume that Michela was expecting guests. This was confirmed when the doorbell rang and three young girls, friends of Michela's, were admitted into the house.

"Go on," said Mrs Murphy. "Go on upstairs, girls. Michela's had the most wonderful news."

Dreading an audience with schoolmates, dreading them seeing him like this, the teasing he would no doubt have to endure, Jacob was nonetheless forced to ferry the refreshments up from the kitchen.

As soon as he nosed his way into the bedroom, the three girls perched on Michela's bed swung round.

"Oh-My-God!" cried Trudy Patterson, a nasty, spiteful,

pigtailed girl who had always acted with incredible hostility towards Jacob. "It's true—Jacob 'piss pants' Fallada is actually your dog."

"Look at the silly little freak," said Kerry Pearson, a quite astonishingly unattractive personality, cut from the same reprehensible cloth as the Patterson girl.

"But when all's said and done," Monica Callas joined in, "he probably looks at this as a promotion—that he's come up in the world. I mean, at least he's not getting his head forced into a dirty toilet bowl or being made to scrape the dried, encrusted snot from off under the desks and eat it."

"Yeah," said Michela. "And he has his uses. Grab those snacks, will you, girls. I'm starved."

As requested, the three friends took everything from the howdah and laid it out on Michela's bed, assembling an extensive picnic on top of the sheets, and for the time being, they lost all interest in Jacob. From down by his basket, he had to lay on the floor and listen to them relay all the school gossip.

"…whether he actually, you know, put it inside her or not, no one can say. But it certainly caused a stir, Michela, I can tell you."

"Oh," said Monica, chomping her way through a mouthful of shop-bought coleslaw, "and at assembly yesterday, the Head told the school that Jacob Fallada was responsible for assaulting you. He actually came out and laid all the blame on that little cretin." She hitched a thumb over her shoulder. "But he assured us he was being punished, that he was undergoing treatment for his 'anti-social behaviour.'"

"And all his artwork has been taken from the art room and destroyed," said Kerry, turning and flashing Jacob a malicious grin. "Other pupils insisted upon it. They didn't feel comfortable having his sketchbooks in Miss Rudd's storeroom. They felt it was, erm…I don't know?—disloyal to you. So, the caretaker tossed the lot on a bonfire."

Jacob's heart sank—his artwork was all he had. And while he never actually shared it with anyone, to know that hours of creative toil, the very best part of himself, had been indiscriminately thrown onto a bonfire with all the winter detritus and burnt by the caretaker depressed him more than he thought possible.

After they'd eaten and drunk their fill, the girls refocused their attention upon Jacob.

"What kinds of things does your new dog do, then, Michela?" asked Trudy, wiping her sticky fingers on her jeans.

"Oh, not much," she said, with a real sense of deflation in her voice, as if Jacob's presence so far had proved incredibly disappointing. "He can roll over, stuff like that. Watch."

Michela ordered Jacob to perform a few rudimentary tricks which summarily failed to impress the other girls.

As if trying to salvage the situation, she added:

"And if he misbehaves in any way, I'm allowed to throw a glass of water in his face."

"Water?" said Trudy, already getting to her feet and heading for the pitcher on the bedside table. "Interesting. Let's give it a go."

After each girl had mumbled an insensible and/or wholly impossible order in Jacob's direction, one he had absolutely no chance of complying with whatever the circumstances, they tossed a full glass of water into his face. But even this, as much as they cackled with laughter, didn't seem to hold their attention for long.

"You know what dogs are really, really good at?" said Monica.

The other girls shook their heads.

"Licking their bum-holes."

This greatly excited all present. Getting to their feet, the three fully able-bodied girls rounded on Jacob, pulling him into the centre of the room, grabbing and grappling with him, manipulating his body, bending him almost in two, forcing his face (his mouth in particular) as close to his buttocks as they possibly could.

"Go on, dog," Trudy panted through her exertions. "Lick your bum."

Grabbing a handful of his hair, Monica screeched into his ear, "Poke your tongue into your arse, she said!"

"Do it!" shouted Kerry, jabbing Jacob hard in the ribs.

In the struggle that followed, he was tempted to fight back, defend himself, defend what little remained of his dignity, to roughly push these horrible creatures away from him, but memory of Mr Murphy's taser quashed any thoughts of an uprising. And, as Trudy pummelled him about the face and chest, he reluctantly prodded his tongue into the seat of his trousers.

"Classic," said Michela, clapping her hands with rhythmical gusto.

"Wait," said Kerry, rummaging around in her rucksack. "Hold him there, Monica. Let me take a few snaps."

With all the studied concentration of a skilled studio photographer, Kerry crouched, moved, crouched, moved, and took a series of photographs of Jacob in this most unflattering and humiliating of poses.

"Look at this one, Jacob." She dangled a Polaroid in front of his eyes, a close-up of his face squashed up against his buttocks. Incredibly, she had taken the pictures with such creative deftness, such skilful use of perspective, it made it look as if Jacob was acting under his own volition, as if he was the only one present.

"Only one place for these," said Trudy, flicking through

the other Polaroids, "school noticeboard."

***

For the next three weeks, Jacob performed his household duties with the desired proficiency and vigour. Through hard experience, he had learned what to do and how to act. Although difficult, he avoided interaction with the devious, cruel and recalcitrant Michela at all costs. As soon as Mr or Mrs Murphy had disenabled the security system, he accompanied the father outside, performed his morning functions, then went back through to the kitchen to transport Michela's breakfast things upstairs. During any free time, he lay huddled up in his basket, trying to remain still and silent, to bring as little attention to himself as possible.

For her part, Michela acted with almost complete indifference towards Jacob now. To her, he was nothing more than an irritant, an impediment. If ever he was a novelty to her and her friends, that novelty had most certainly worn off. Now that she was mobile and self-sufficient once again, she simply kneed her way past him if he got in her way or clouted him unceremoniously around the head. In fact, it had gotten to the point, now that her return to school was imminent, where she openly requested that Jacob leave the household altogether.

"I understand, darling," said Mr Murphy. "Won't be long now. But we wouldn't want to jeopardise the integrity of our study now, would we?"

Two more days passed.

Jacob, having kept a firm track of the passing time, knew that the three weeks was almost up. When he was called down to the front room, therefore, he hoped that this would indeed be the day that he regained his freedom.

"Now, Jacob," said Mr Murphy. "We have come to the end of our experiment. I'm pleased to say, after a decidedly poor start, your behaviour and application improved so immeasurably, that we are pleased to award you the mark of 'satisfactory.'" He raised both hands, as if anticipating some kind of protest or challenge from Jacob. "I know you might find that a little harsh. I know you might've had your heart set on a 'distinction', but I'm afraid, due to the fact that we had to result to not only water aversion therapy but use of the taser, that just isn't possible."

There was a brief silence. Mr Murphy turned and looked at his wife over her shoulder, as if her expression was the most accurate gauge of his performance so far.

He returned to Jacob, "In a few minutes, your aunt is going to come and collect you. I've printed her off a copy of our interim report. Any amendments we make will be forwarded in the post. So, whenever you're ready, Jacob, feel free to stand up, stretch your legs, roll your neck, whatever you feel like doing. You're free to go home now."

But when Jacob tried to stand and straighten, his body simply wouldn't comply—he found it impossible to get to his feet, to do anything other than remain on the floor like the dog he had been for the last twenty-one days.

"Jacob?" said Mr Murphy, a hint of concern in his voice now. "What's wrong?"

But he couldn't reply, he couldn't speak or move, no matter how hard he tried to engage his tongue.

Mr Murphy took a few tentative steps forward.

"Please, Jacob, you must—" the doorbell cut him short.

"What are we going to do?" asked Mrs Murphy.

"I…I don't know."

The doorbell sounded for a second time.

Husband and wife exchanged a quick, anxious glance.

"You, erm…better get that, darling. We can't keep Ms Fallada waiting all day now, can we?"

A few moments later, Jacob's aunt walked into the front room.

"Hello, Jacob," she said, eyeing him on the floor there, a confused look on her face, not really knowing what was taking place. "What...whatever is wrong with the boy?"

She turned and looked at Mr and Mrs Murphy who shrugged and smiled awkwardly, as if they too were baffled by his strange behaviour.

"Jacob," said his aunt in much sterner tones. "Stand up, I say. You're making an exhibition of yourself."

But he still couldn't do it, still he couldn't move or speak. Which only angered his aunt all the more.

"Jacob Fallada, stand up this instant. Stop behaving so rudely." She shook her head and clicked her tongue. "You've always been such an awkward boy, the bane of my life. You don't know how relaxing it's been these last few weeks, not having you around the house."

In frustration, she aimed a kick at Jacob that went glancing off his knee.

"Please, Ms Fallada," said Mr Murphy, stepping forward. "We won't tolerate any physical abuse under our roof. I'm sure he'll be fine soon." He put one hand on her shoulder and offered her a thick wad of bound papers with the other. "Here's a copy of our report."

But she wasn't really listening.

"Report?" she mouthed absently, still staring hard at Jacob.

"Yes, our report on Jacob's conduct, the findings of our social-behavioural experiment."

"What?" She waved his words away and moved closer to Jacob, ducking down, taking hold of his chin and turning his head right and left. "But...but it's as if he's nothing more than a stupid bloody dog now."

3

Of Christians and Cannibals

Jacob Fallada had been so absorbed in his artistic work, hunched over a sketchbook, he didn't realise that the café's stony-faced proprietor was now standing by his table.

"Excuse me, son."

Startled, Jacob whisked the sketchbook out of sight, concealing it on his lap.

"Yes."

"Do you know how long you've been sitting here, over one simple cup of coffee?"

Jacob blinked in confusion.

"Let me tell you: three hours and fourteen minutes. And do you know how much that equates to per minute, per grain of bloody coffee?"

"I—"

"It equates to bankruptcy for me, that's what." He threw up his hands and brought them slapping back down by his sides. "I can't afford to have you sitting at one of my prime window seats all day, scribbling in your notebook. This isn't a bloody library or art room, you know, it's a place of business."

"But—"

"But nothing! I've had my eye on you for weeks, said to myself, next time I see that scruffy streak of shit, I'm going to tell him what's what, that we don't need his kind of custom, a piss-taker taking the piss out of the facilities. So, as of now, you're barred from my establishment. Understand?"

Jacob felt his heart sink. Over the last year or so, ever since the public library had closed due to a lack of funding, this quaint little café with the beautiful sea views had become his own peaceful refuge, a place he could take his sketchbook and notepad and absorb himself in his artistic work for hours, unmolested by his aunt, people, the outside world in general.

"I said: do you understand?"

Briefly, Jacob felt like arguing, telling the proprietor that, granted, he may not be the biggest of spenders, that he may not come in and order a lavish three-course meal, but he was a regular patron, that his daily cup of coffee added up over the months, and that at this hour of the day the café was almost always deserted, that there were rarely ever families waiting to sit at any of the four prime window seats, but the proprietor looked too angry, too agitated, as if Jacob's very existence was a personal affront to him and everything he stood for.

"Yes," he said, gathering up his things. "I understand."

Once outside, Jacob felt a gloomy depression set in. Reluctant to return to a home that wasn't really his own, he decided to roam the now-dark small-town streets, to collect his thoughts, to focus his mind on finding a new location to conduct his artistic work in the future, somewhere remote, removed, where he wouldn't risk coming into contact with nasty little people and their almost pathological dislike for him.

Lost in impotent thought, he was about to cross the road near the churchyard when he heard a pitiful moan.

Curious, he turned around and peered into the shadows.

Sprawled across a wooden bench, head lolling to the side, limbs splayed, as if suffering from injury or illness that required immediate medical attention, was what looked like a young woman.

Jacob walked over to investigate.

He was right.

In her early twenties, with dark tangled hair, much of it covering her face, the prostrate female wore a short, figure-hugging dress and high-heeled shoes. Due to the awkward angle in which she lay slumped, the dress had ridden up, revealing the tops of her shapely thighs and a hint of lacy black underwear.

Averting his eyes, Jacob crouched in front of her, spying an empty bottle of vodka mired in a pool of thick vomit. In the past, he had heard about this kind of drunkenness, read newspaper articles about disenfranchised young people who regularly sought oblivion through excessive alcohol intake. He knew, therefore, the dangers associated with binge-drinking, choking on vomit being the most perilous.

"Are you all right?" he asked, covering his nose as the harsh stench of sick hit his nostrils.

She didn't respond—not in coherent words, anyway. She shifted slightly, mumbled, and raised a shaky hand, as if trying to bring Jacob's attention to something directly behind him. But when he turned his head, all he saw was the empty pavement and adjoining roadway bathed in street-light orange.

"My name's Jacob Fallada," he almost shouted, as if talking to someone with impaired hearing. "I really think you should get home now. Would you like me to hail you a taxi?"

This time she didn't respond at all.

He darted another look over his shoulder, hoping that somebody much better equipped to deal with the situation might be passing. But all he saw were the same empty pavements and bright orange street lights.

Resolved to help, to not leave a poor defenceless young woman to a dubious fate, he shook her shoulder, swept the thick matted hair from her eyes and lightly slapped her face. But again, she barely responded.

"Right, I'm going to try and help you to stand up now," he said, grabbing her under the arms and lifting her up from the bench.

Incredibly, her rubbery limbs responded. With one of her arms draped over his shoulders, one of his clasped around her waist, supporting the majority of her weight, he managed to walk her over to the side of the road.

But before he could even look up the street for an oncoming taxi, a sharp, challenging female voice rang out from the shadows of the night:

"What do you think you're doing?"

Both startled and overjoyed at this development, Jacob slowly shuffled himself and his drunken ward around to where that voice had emanated from.

"Thank God." He singularly failed to mask his relief as a man and woman made their way over to them. "I was just passing through town when I found this young woman sprawled across a bench. I think she's had far too much to drink. I—"

"You didn't answer my question."

For a second time that evening, Jacob blinked in confusion, puzzled not just by her words but confrontational tone.

"What?"

"No, you didn't," said her companion, a hulking, dangerous-looking individual with a shaven head and monstrous biceps bulging through a tight leather bomber jacket. "What are you doing here, in town, now, with her?"

"Erm, I'm just a local artist out for a stroll."

"You what?" he said, stepping forward, puffing out his considerable chest. "You're an artist, are you?"

"That's right," said Jacob, adjusting his somewhat precarious hold on the woman, being careful not to lose his grip and send her crashing to the pavement. "A few minutes ago, I found the young lady here, on a bench, semi-conscious, moaning and groaning. And I wanted to make sure she got home unharmed."

Even though Jacob felt as if he had just described the situation clearly and unequivocally, the couple looked far from convinced.

"I don't know, Steve," the woman turned and said to her companion. "I don't like the look of this. She's completely off her face, out of it, don't know which day of the week it is… And look, her dress has been pulled right up, you can see her knickers." She knelt before the young woman and tugged her dress down to cover her underwear. "I bet this bastard got her into this state. I bet he was planning on—"

"What?" cried Jacob. "Don't be so ridiculous!"

"Is that what you did, pal?" said Steve. "Took advantage of that young girl in some bar, did you? Slipped something into her drink, a Mickey Finn, while she nipped to the toilets, then dragged her out here?"

"No! Of course not. I—"

"Shut it!" shouted the woman, glaring at Jacob over her shoulder. "Not another word out of you. If he opens his mouth again, Steve, wallop the bastard."

"With pleasure, Gladys, with bloody pleasure." And Steve stepped in between Jacob and the pavement, blocking any potential escape route.

Gladys stood and straightened, put a hand on the drunken girl's shoulder, and spoke slowly and loudly into her ear.

"Are you all right, love? Had a bit too much to drink, eh? Don't worry. We're here now. We won't let anything bad happen to you."

Nudging Jacob out of the way, Gladys took hold of the drunken girl's arm, and carefully sat her down on the church wall.

"What'd you think we should do?" asked Steve.

"Call the police, nothing else for it. If we hadn't have come along, God knows what would've happened."

Jacob rubbed both hands up and down his face. He knew exactly what these people were accusing him of but had no idea how to convince them otherwise.

"Look," he said. "I was merely trying to help. I just wanted to make sure she was all right. I—"

"I bet you did," said Gladys, jabbing a forefinger in Jacob's direction. "See it on the news all the time—bloody date rapists. Bet you would've loved to have gotten your hands on a semi-comatose girl, wouldn't you, eh? Don't have to worry about consent or getting knocked back then, do you? Huh! Your kind disgusts me."

"My kind?"

"Yeah, your kind—scruffy, grubby perverts, sex fiends, paedophiles."

As Gladys listed further undesirable elements she now associated with Jacob, two young women walked over to the side of the road. Both wore stylish trouser suits, as if they had just left the office after a late meeting.

"What's going on?" the taller, darker-haired of the two asked. "What's happened?"

Gladys stepped forward.

"We just caught that piece of shit over there"—again, she thrust an accusing forefinger in Jacob's direction—"about to sexually assault this poor young lass. Looks like date rape, that he slipped something into her drink and—"

"Wait just a minute!" cried Jacob. "You did nothing of the sort." He turned to the newcomers. "Five minutes ago, I, very innocently, walked past a bench in the churchyard and saw the young lady there"—he hitched a thumb over his shoulder—"in clear distress. I tried to speak to her, but she was far too intoxicated to respond. Concerned for her welfare, I attempted to hail her a—"

"Cor!" spat Gladys. "You've got your cover story off pat, ain't yer? When me and Steve got here, he was all over that vulnerable girl, her skirt was up round her neck. He were like a wild bloody animal."

"That's simply not true," said Jacob, bewildered by these blatant untruths and baseless accusations.

"It does look pretty bad, though," said the shorter, slighter, softer spoken of the two women. "I mean, what are you doing out here, at night, on a park bench, next to a woman who's clearly been drugged in some way? Who are you? What do you do for living?"

"A living?" said Jacob, struggling to take all of this in, to understand quite how he'd got himself into this awful position. "I'm an artist."

"An artist?" she said, doubtfully. "Everybody says that, don't they?—especially those from the deviant classes. And you do hear about this type of thing a lot these days: men drugging women in pubs and clubs, bundling them into the back of a taxi, and taking them to some seedy flea-pit, dark alleyway or convenient churchyard to subject them to all kinds of abominations."

"Exactly," said Gladys, nodding enthusiastically. "I'm just glad we came along in the nick of time."

"Look," said Jacob, resolving to put up a full defence of himself. "I've done nothing wrong. I can assure you." Again he addressed himself to the two young women. "When they walked over, I wasn't attacking anyone—far from it. I was—"

"Only because we startled you," said Gladys. "Jesus! He had his prick halfway out of his trousers, didn't he, Steve?"

"Yep. Looked that way to me."

Jacob was too appalled to speak, to even attempt to refute such a preposterous claim.

"So, what are we going to do?" asked the dark-haired woman. "We can't leave him alone with her. We've got to do something."

"Call the police," said Gladys. "Wait until they get here. Tell them what we saw. Then let them deal with him."

"The police?" said Jacob, truly worried now. Never had he been in any trouble with the authorities before. "That's completely unnecessary. What you claim to have seen never took place. You're making a huge mistake. In fact, I challenge you to call 999. That way, I can explain myself in full. That way, the young woman over there will be taken care of, and I can get off home to continue with my artistic work."

Gladys scowled and took her mobile phone from her pocket. "Grab a hold of him, Steve. Make sure he doesn't do a bunk. I'm calling the Old Bill."

Steve did as instructed. Jacob, therefore, had not only to endure a barrage of wrongful accusations, but also to be manhandled, forced into a hugely effective and uncomfortable headlock.

Twenty minutes later, a police car arrived at the scene. By then, a sizeable crowd of onlookers had gathered. One by one, Gladys told each individual her own skewed version of events. Whenever Jacob tried to protest his innocence, Steve squeezed his neck a little harder, forcing the words straight back into his mouth.

Two tall, broad-shouldered police officers got out of the car.

"Good evening, I'm P.C. Collings. This is my colleague P.C. James. What seems to be the problem here?"

"Date rape," Gladys rushed over and told them. "Me and my fella were on our way to the curry house when we stumbled upon that pervert over there. Clearly, he'd drugged the young girl now sitting on the wall and was about to have his wicked way with her, his trousers were round his ankles and he was—he was, you know, sexually aroused."

Collings looked over to Steve, only then realising that Jacob, the accused man, was being forcibly restrained

"Okay, sir," said the policeman. "Let the chap go now, will you? We'll take care of things from here on out."

Reluctantly, Steve released his grip.

Gasping for breath, Jacob stood, straightened, and rubbed his neck.

"Officers, thank God," he panted. "This has all been a terrible misunderstanding."

"No it hasn't," said Gladys. "Don't listen to him. If we hadn't have come along when we did, he'd have probably raped that young girl, cut her throat, and made off into the night. All he's been going on about is—"

"Okay, okay," said P.C. James, stepping forward of his colleague. "Please, calm down now, madam. Sir"—he turned to Jacob—"can you give us your version of events now, please?"

"Yes, yes, of course." And Jacob told him everything. He told him about the hours he spent in the local café sketching out ideas for a new artistic project, how he'd fancied a stroll afterwards, a breath of fresh air, how he'd heard the girl moaning and groaning, and how he'd tried to help her, getting her to her feet in an attempt to hail her a taxi, everything up until the moment that the policemen themselves had arrived.

"So, you're an artist, you say?"

Jacob nodded.

"And do you have any identification, a bank card or driver's licence?"

But Jacob had neither—he had no bank account and had never learned to drive. As far as he was concerned, financial institutions were the embodiment of the evils of modern society, and the motor car responsible for the devastation of the planet's environment. More importantly, cards and licences were infringements upon his personal freedoms, both as citizen and artist. Therefore, he carried nothing on his person to verify his identity.

"No, I'm afraid not. I live what you might call a bohemian existence. I don't believe that a person should have to carry around a card with all their personal details on it."

"He's taking the piss!" Gladys spluttered. "Trying to wriggle out of things, failing to cooperate, playing for time. Course he's got some i.d. on him. Search him, get him down the station—only place for a conniving bastard like him."

"Please, madam," said Collings. "You're not helping."

"Don't you 'Please madam' me. I won't just sit back and watch as he mugs you off, making you look like incompetent fools."

The policeman scowled and stamped his foot—clearly aspersions towards his professional conduct were tantamount to a mortal insult.

"Madam, I won't tell you again. We're trying to ascertain exactly what took place here this evening. So kindly keep your comments to yourself. If not, we'll have no other option than to charge you with wasting police time."

"'Wasting police time'!—of all the cheek. We've just done your bloody job for you, caught a date rapist, red-handed, bang to rights. And you stand there talking about—"

"Shush, hey, Glad," Steve talked over her, took her arm, and drew her aside. "Let the officers take care of things, eh?"

Collings nodded at him gratefully and then returned to Jacob.

"Okay, sir. So you claim to have no identification on your person. But if we need to take the matter further, and by that I mean confirm your name, date of birth, and place of residence, I take it you won't withhold that information from us?"

"Of course not. For the record, my name is Jacob Fallada, I'm twenty-one years old and reside here in town with my aunt."

"Thank you," said Collings. "Most helpful. Now, can I ask you what you've got under your arm?"

"This?" Jacob withdrew the almost forgotten sketchbook. "Just my artistic work, the things I was working on in the café earlier."

"And would you mind if we had a look inside, sir?"

"Erm, I'd rather you didn't," said Jacob, in all seriousness. He hated the idea of showing his artistic work to anyone. "Not that I've got anything to hide, it's just not something I'd feel very comfortable with. Besides, these sketches and so forth are completely irrelevant to the situation at hand."

"We'll be the judge of that, sir."

"Yeah, we will," said the dark-haired woman in the trouser suit. "I think you should check the folder, officer. Maybe he's got his date rape drugs stashed away in there."

"Don't be so absurd!" said Jacob, holding up the sketchbook, turning it around in his hands, patting each side, showcasing its pancake-flat dimensions. "There's nothing in here but sheets of paper. Anyone can see that."

"Wouldn't hurt to check, though," said Steve, sheepishly, perhaps fearful of a similar reprimand to Gladys'.

"No, really, I'm going to have to insist," said Jacob. "I've done nothing wrong. I don't deserve to be treated like a criminal when all I tried to do was help."

"I understand that, sir," said P.C. James. "But you must appreciate the position we as police officers find ourselves in. Earlier, we received an emergency call regarding a rape in progress. Several witnesses"—he gestured to the dozen or so people looking on—"claim that they interrupted you in the midst of a serious sexual assault. We have to investigate this matter fully. You see that, don't you, sir?"

Jacob nodded reluctantly. He couldn't argue with anything the policeman had just said.

"So why not hand us the sketchbook, eh?" He reached out a hand, only for Jacob to take a step back, whisking it away.

"Oh, just give him the bloody thing," cried Gladys, making a wild grab for the sketchbook.

"No!" Jacob cried, tugging it back with one hand, and pushing her away with the other.

"Give it to me! Give it to me!"

As a fierce tug-of-war struggle ensued, as the policeman tried to separate the two antagonists, the drunken woman suddenly shouted:

"Stop!"

So unexpected was her revival, everyone who had been involved in the fracas did indeed stop, turn around and face her.

"Look," said Gladys. "She's…She's awake."

Both policemen walked over to the wall.

"Are you all right, young lady?" asked P.C. James.

She swallowed hard, nodded, and wiped the back of her hand across her lips.

"Got a throbbing headache and a dry mouth, but I'll survive." She tried to smile. "Self-inflicted, so I can't be looking for nobody's sympathy."

"Self-inflicted?" said Collings. "How'd you mean?"

"I, erm…had a bit of a rough day. I…I bought a bottle of cheap vodka and decided to sit here and get off my face. Stupid, I know. But things just got on top of me, that's all."

Collings gestured towards Jacob.

"Madam, can you cast your mind back to earlier this evening, before you passed out. Did this man attack you?"

She shook her head. "No, no. He came over a little while back. I remember him trying to talk to me. He was really nice, kind, he tried to help me out, he tried to get me over to the side of the road to hail a cab."

"Ha!" Jacob was unable to contain himself. He went right up to Gladys and Steve and jabbed his own forefinger in their faces. "You see? You see?" He swung round to the crowds of people looking on. "All I did was try and help someone in dire straits, acting with kindness and consideration, and what do I get for it: a rape accusation, physical assault, the threat of arrest."

"I…I know what I saw," said Gladys, unrepentant, but in far from convincing tones.

Jacob shook his head.

"Officers"—he walked over to the policemen—"I demand that those two over there be arrested for slander and wrongful accusations. They knew I'd done nothing wrong, but still they—"

"That's not going to happen, sir," said Collings. "And I think you know that."

"What? But they tried to have me arrested for drug rape. If the young lady hadn't have come round when she did, you would undoubtedly have taken me into custody. Things could've snowballed. I could've spent years in prison for a crime I didn't commit. They made up a pack of lies about me, they…Surely they can't just get away with it?"

"An unfortunate misunderstanding, sir," said P.C. James. "Like you, these two citizens were only looking out for the young lady's welfare." He pointed to the crowd of onlookers. "Okay you lot, off you go now, nothing more to see here, let's be having you."

As the crowds dispersed, Jacob, his anger softening into relief, sidled up alongside the policemen.

"And what about the young woman now, officers?" he asked. "She's still in a bit of a state. No doubt you can drop her home. After everything that's happened, it would put my mind at rest to know that she has, at the very least, got back to her place of residence safely."

This proposition seemed to amuse them.

"Why are you laughing?" asked Jacob, offended by their reaction.

"We're not a taxi service," said P.C. James. "If she's stupid enough to get herself into that state, she'll have to suffer the consequences."

"What?" Jacob had never heard anything so preposterous in his entire life. Surely the emergency services should endeavour to assist every vulnerable individual they come across. "But she's still unsteady on her feet, barely conscious, in fact, she might freeze to death out here, be robbed, set upon, assaulted in the violent manner I was accused of earlier. You can't just leave her like this."

"Yes we can, and fully intend to do so, sir." He patted Jacob's shoulder in a cold, completely patronising manner. "Good evening, Mr Fallada."

With that, the policemen got into their car and drove away.

"Sorry for all the trouble I've caused," said the young woman.

Jacob turned and walked over to the church wall.

"Don't worry," he said, sitting next to her. "It's not your fault. But what are you going to do now? Get a taxi? Walk home?"

She shook her head. "I…I don't think I can make it on my own." Breathing hard, she buried her head in her hands.

"Oh, don't cry," said Jacob, patting her back.

"I'm not," she replied, slowly lifting her head. "I'm just trying to get myself together." She hesitated. "Look. Can I ask you for one last favour?"

"Of course."

"Could you help me to the bus stop over there?" She pointed across the road. "The number forty-four goes right by my flat. Any luck, one should be passing in a few minutes."

"Right, yes, good idea."

"Thanks so much." She smiled warmly at him. "My name's Rachel, by the way."

"Jacob." He shook the soft clammy hand she offered. "Whenever you're ready, Rachel, we'll get you across that road."

Like before, her rubbery limbs somehow responded.

With one of her arms draped over his shoulders, one of his clasped around her waist, they managed to get to the other side of the road just as a bus pulled up at the stop.

"Great," said Jacob, skipping over to the automatic door as it clattered open. "Hello there," he said to the driver. "My friend here has been taken unwell. Would it be okay if I helped her aboard and found her a seat? I won't be accompanying her on the journey. I just want to make sure she gets on okay."

The driver didn't look very impressed but nodded his assent, anyway.

Jacob helped Rachel clamber aboard, walking her all the way down the centre aisle to the last unoccupied pair of seats.

"Right," he said, carefully depositing her on the seat nearest the window. "You'll be all right from here on out. I'll tell the driver to call you when your—" to Jacob's horror, the bus rumbled into life, pulling away from the side of the road.

In panic, he thought about shouting out and jabbing a finger at the red stop button, but quickly realised how futile that would be, that he was somehow destined not to get home until the early hours of the morning; that this small part of his life story was not to be a successful or very happy one.

Too weary to battle fate, he slumped down in the seat next to Rachel and ran both hands through his thick, straggly hair.

"What are you up to?" a sharp, challenging female voice jolted Jacob back into the here and now.

He looked up to see a hideously fat, hard-faced couple glaring over the seats directly in front of him.

"I said: what are you up to?" the woman repeated.

"Erm, I…" Jacob trailed off and looked at Rachel for support, but she was fast asleep, unconscious, her head lolling to the side.

"That young girl don't look to be in very good shape to me," said the man. "What'd you do to her, eh?—slip something into her drink in some seedy bar or nightclub? A Micky-Bloody-Finn. Looking to get her back to your place, are you? Looking to take advantage while she's off her face?"

4

Promise Me No Promises

Jacob Fallada leaned back on a park bench, closed his eyes, and listened to the familiar yet somehow disconcerting sounds of children at play: the shrieks, excited voices and high-pitched laughter. It took him back to his own childhood, to those dark, confusing days where all he sought was peace, quiet, and solitude, where this kind of raucous scene was pure torture, a rolling kind of purgatory he could never quite escape. It's odd, he thought to himself, how something so synonymous with innocence, the happiest, most carefree times of life were associated with his own bleakest memories, the most sickening of emotions, as if his sensory apparatus had been reversed, as if black was white, as if he were subject to a completely different set of emotional criteria than ordinary, everyday people. And although he could easily identify the root causes for this, he still wasn't sure why he had been destined to feel so isolated and conflicted all the time.

When he opened his eyes again, he was startled to see someone standing right in front of him, a slender, casually dressed yet decidedly smart, well-to-do woman in her late twenties.

"I'm sorry, but I really need to have a word with you."

"Me?"

"That's right. I'm a young mother. My two children are playing just over there in the sandpit." She gestured towards the sun-drenched play area. "Over the last few weeks, I've seen you down here a hell of a lot. And I don't like it one bit."

Jacob blinked in confusion. He had no idea what this woman was trying to say. This was, after all, a public place, a place he had come to frequent in the summer months, to sketch, jot down notes, read, relax, gather his thoughts. He had as much right to be here as anybody else.

"I am, in fact, speaking on behalf of a dozen or so concerned mothers who don't like the idea of such an unkempt loner staring at their children for hours on end, who don't want to put them at risk of being accosted by someone who could very well be on the sex register."

Only then did Jacob realise exactly why she had approached him.

"Now, we don't want to have to call the police. But if you don't leave here, this minute, I'll be forced to—"

"Maureen, no," said a petite, middle-aged woman in glasses, who had literally appeared out of nowhere. "Not to be clichéd, but you're barking up the wrong tree. This young man is an artist. I've seen him down here with his sketchbook countless times before. I've sat next to him on this very bench, and he didn't even know I was there, so absorbed was he in his drawing. He isn't some deviant stalking local children. If anything, you're the one harassing him, interrupting his work."

Maureen's cheeks reddened; she became incredibly flustered, incredibly quickly.

"Oh, my word. I…I'm terribly sorry." She swallowed hard and shifted her weight. "It's just…it's just that you hear such awful things these days, and, not to be rude, but you look so, so down-at-the-heel, pretty much like every mother's worst nightmare. I just assumed you were a…a, you know."

So effusive were her apologetic words, so horrified did she look at her mistake, Jacob found himself apologising in return, just as effusively, saying that he understood perfectly well why she had reacted in the way she did, almost conceding the fact that he did indeed resemble the popular image of a career paedophile.

"Really, it's nothing," he assured her, "a misunderstanding, just one of those things."

After graciously accepting his apology, Maureen scuttled away, joining a group of young mothers gathered by the climbing-frames, no doubt awaiting a full account of her exchange with the dubious stranger who had so enflamed their maternal anxiety.

Jacob turned to the woman in glasses.

"Thank you for that," he said, ruefully shaking his head. "For interceding, I mean. I don't know what it is, but that kind of thing happens to me quite often."

"It's because you're different," she said, carefully folding her pretty floral-print dress and sitting next to him. "It's because you're an artist, someone who lives an alternative lifestyle that everyday people just can't understand. Normal Joes and Josephines fear those who want to create, express themselves, who are not driven by money and material possessions. Put simply, your mere existence makes them question theirs."

Jacob took a moment to consider her words. Not one to overthink things too much, the reasons why he did what he did, he nonetheless thought she had summed up his situation, and that of anyone who seeks to be creative in the modern world, to dedicate themselves to an artform, particularly well indeed. For that reason, he felt an instant connection, a bond, a sense of solidarity. Rarely had anyone taken the time to try and understand him, his way of life and motivations.

"I, myself, am a bit of a weekend artist," she told him. "Not that my work is easy to define, categorise, put into any kind of box. I tend to splice genres, mix things up—part painter, part writer, part candlestick maker."

"Really?" said Jacob, laughing at her amusing play on words.

"Yes. In fact, I was thinking of taking my sketchbook down to the promenade tomorrow morning, near where the fishing boats are moored overnight. Not to be presumptuous, but would you like to perhaps meet up? We could carry on our discussion about art and artists, why we spend all our time in front of a canvas or hunched over a sheet of writing paper."

"Erm, yes," he replied, a little wrong-footed by her suggestion—strangers rarely spoke to him, let alone made arrangements for a second meeting. "Yes, I would."

"Good." She smiled and got to her feet. "I'll see you then…then. Ha! Oh, and my name's Rhea, by the way."

Shyly, she offered him a slender hand with black painted nails to shake.

"And I'm Jacob, Jacob Fallada."

That night, Jacob found it almost impossible to sleep. He

was far too excited by what amounted to both a regulation date and an artistic assignation with an incredibly intriguing woman. Perhaps this whole thing was fated, he thought to himself.

Perhaps I was destined to be in the park at that precise hour of the morning. Perhaps, perversely, being accused of being a potential child rapist was part of the whole karmic process, to bring me closer to Rhea, a fellow artist, someone who understands the inner workings of my mind, someone I can talk to freely and openly, perhaps even show my own body of work. Perhaps all the pain and rejection of my early life was leading up to this one point.

In this irrepressible state, he tried to remember every aspect of Rhea's appearance: the dark, tangled hair that rested at a shoulder's length, the pale, almost porcelain skin, the curious greeny-blue eyes that lurked behind her stylish designer glasses, the quite disarming white-toothed smile, petite, almost painfully thin frame, which belied the dynamo-like energy generated by what clearly was a fierce intelligence, the simple floral dress, shoes with straps, the black nail polish. All in all, Jacob Fallada had never met anyone like Rhea before.

Next morning, he made his way down to the promenade at the appointed time. It was another fine, if slightly overcast day. In the shifting sunshine, fishermen in oilskins sat around on improvised stools made of plastic fish crates, darning crab-pots with thick hempen rope. Seagulls squawked. Dogs raced along the shoreline, chasing tennis balls or sticks and barking at the odd unsuspecting jogger.

"Jacob, over here." Rhea waved at him from the seawall.

He walked over to find her resplendent in a navy-blue dress with a white Peter Pan collar.

"I'm not late, am I?" he asked

"No, not at all, right on time. Take a seat. It's another wonderful day. And I so love the smell of sea air in the morning. And it's so quaint around here, isn't it?—like something from a bygone age."

"Yes. Yes, it is."

But in truth, this part of town had always depressed Jacob. The beach huts were boarded-up and vandalised, coonskin cap wearing wastrels often sprawled out on benches with truly enormous bottles of super-strength cider, the beach itself was made up of big banks of shingle and stone rather than fine golden sand, and the air was tainted with a mixture of engine oil and fish guts. But perhaps, if Jacob was being honest, his antipathy towards the area was due to the fact that the most unedifying incident from his childhood took place not twenty or so yards from where he had just sat down.

"There you go," said Rhea, handing him a cup of coffee from a flask. "I thought we could sit and talk as opposed to work. In fact, I thought you might like to see my old portfolio."

To his surprise, she had brought a stack of sketchbooks and an old portfolio from her younger art school days.

"I…I'd be delighted," said Jacob, keen to get an insight into Rhea's character through her work. "I didn't think to bring anything of mine with me, though. Truth be told, I rarely if ever show people my work. Even now, after all these years of solitary artistic toil, I…I don't think I'm quite ready."

"I understand," she said, opening the portfolio and placing it on his lap.

It was a contrary experience: seeing Rhea's (or anyone else's) artwork for the very first time, to flick through the glossy, professional portfolio and a few of her sketchbooks.

While she was a more than competent draughtswoman, each and every one of her pictures (and the subject matter was undoubtedly original and arresting: slithers of tattooed skin crawling across a canvas, housewives masturbating in incredibly well-rendered domestic scenes: the laundry room, the kitchen while saucepans overflowed with boiling water, photographs of Rhea in the throes of creating street art in a city Jacob didn't recognise) lacked that indefinable, elusive sense of originality, spark, character, soul, the one thing each and every artist sets out to achieve. They were bland in their very outlandishness. And he felt, not so much disappointed with Rhea, but sympathetic, that for all her efforts—and this was clearly after years and years of artistic endeavour (no one could have assembled a portfolio this extensive without real dedication)—she perhaps wasn't all that talented.

"So, what do you think?" she asked with such eagerness, and in such close proximity now (as he flicked from page to page, picture to picture, she had edged ever closer) it made Jacob feel incredibly uncomfortable.

"I really like them," he embellished more than slightly. "I like them all. You're clearly an accomplished and original artist. I could easily see your work exhibited in a big gallery one day."

His reaction, as insincere as it had been, couldn't have thrilled Rhea more. She squealed with delight, took both of his hands in hers, and confessed as to how nervous she had been last night, about showing a fellow artist work she had kept hidden away at home for many years. With almost manic enthusiasm, she opened sketchbook after sketchbook, and showed him other pictures, other samples of her writing, most of it no more than preliminary sketches or rudimentary outlines.

"And this is part of an old project I was hoping to resurrect concerning parental, erm…alienation." She hesitated for a moment and swallowed hard. "An area of great interest to me. If all goes well, I plan to have lots of different images of schoolchildren fading in and out of each other à la Charles Blackman…on big sweeping canvases, with all these childish squiggles, you know, like kids scrape on desks with protractors, or write on walls in felt pens: *Jane loves Arthur, or I woz here*. But to have, instead, really profound statements about the human condition, like: *Promises are harsher than lies*."

"*Promises are harsher than lies*?"

"Yes." She nodded vigorously. "Perhaps it's something we could collaborate on, Jacob."

"Collaborate?" he said, like he had no idea what the word meant, so tiring had this whole performance been, trying to offer so much positive and constructive comment.

"Tell you what, why don't you come around to my place tonight? It's nothing special, just a modest flat on the other side of town. I'll cook you a meal and we can discuss things properly."

That evening, Jacob knocked on her front door, holding a cheap bottle of wine that a distant relative had sent him last Christmas.

"Come in, come in." Rhea greeted him with what Jacob took as a more than affectionate kiss on the cheek.

Contrary to what she had said before, her home was more open-plan-living-space-cum-artist's-studio than "modest flat", with stacks of canvases piled up against white-washed walls and an easel erected under a ceiling light with a work-in-progress on it, what looked like one of the paintings of schoolchildren that she had talked about this morning.

"Ignore that," she said, even though it had clearly been

put there for a purpose, so it was the first thing he saw when he walked through the door. "I hope you're hungry. I've cooked up a bit of a vegetarian feast. Is that okay with you?—a meat-free dinner, I mean."

"Yes, that's fine," said Jacob. While having no ethical convictions whatsoever, the substandard, heavily processed fare that had sustained him since early childhood contained so little actual meat his was probably closer to a vegetarian diet, anyway.

"Excellent." She clapped her hands together. "Now, please, sit at the table. There's a bottle of wine open. Let's eat, drink, and talk about this big collaboration project."

But no sooner had Jacob sat down than Rhea slipped into a strange, distracted, taciturn, almost melancholy mood. Despite her invitation, and effusiveness on his arrival, she didn't seem particularly pleased to see him anymore, to want any company at all tonight. And this happened in a matter of minutes.

And it was only as she served the first course that he found out why.

"Jacob," she said, eyes lowered, light from the flickering candles casting dancing shapes upon her downcast face, "I've been a bit on edge since we met this morning."

"On edge? How do you mean?"

"Well, I've not really met many other artists lately—had the kind of lofty conversation we had earlier. For years now, I've longed to meet likeminded people, to have someone I can bounce ideas off, someone I can show my work to and vice versa."

"I know exactly what you mean," he said. "Ours, unfortunately, is very a solitary existence."

"Exactly. And with you being a local artist, and me being a local artist, and the fact that we get on so well, that there's obviously a strong mutual attraction, means it's only natural that we will spend a lot of time together."

Jacob gave a start.

"Don't look so shocked." She smiled, weakly, or so Jacob thought at the time. "I'm certain you felt it, too, right?"

He nodded but couldn't quite bring himself to look her in the eyes.

"It's so powerful, Jacob—our connection. But if we are to continue seeing each other—which I dearly want to do—there are a few things I need to tell you about my past life."

In slow, considered tones, Rhea told Jacob that she had been previously married, that the relationship had soured to the extent that she had a complete mental breakdown ("and I mean a complete breakdown—sectioned, pumped full of medication, the works") and that after the divorce her ex-husband was granted sole custody of their two children.

"Now they're in their teenage years, and they…they don't want to see me. Marc has turned them against me, you see, has told them some horrendous lies about the past, why I didn't see them very much when they were younger. For that reason, they've completely shunned me, won't so much as speak to me on the telephone or reply to my letters. It's heart-breaking, Jacob, knowing that you have two beautiful children out in the big wide world but they'd rather you didn't exist."

He couldn't have been more moved by her story. Not just the emotion in her voice or the tears that streamed down her cheeks so heavily she had to take off her glasses and dab her eyes with a napkin, but that she had chosen to share it with him after knowing him for such a short time. It showed how much she thought of him already.

"The upshot of which means I have no way of communicating my feelings to them, the sorrow I feel for missing out on so much of their lives. That's why this series of paintings is so important to me. And that's why I'd like to have a collaborator, someone I trust implicitly, someone who can offer support and guidance as I try and reach out to my babies in the only way I know how." She dabbed her eyes with the napkin again. "So, Jacob, will you help me?"

"Yes. Yes, of course, I'd love to."

Next morning, they started working together. At dead on seven o'clock, Rhea met Jacob at the front door in a pair of navy-blue overalls and with her hair tied up in a messy bunch.

"Okay, Jacob," she said, taking his hand. "I sorted through everything last night, all my old canvases, preliminary sketches, notebooks, and suchlike. Come. I'll show you."

She walked him over to a large, half-completed canvas daubed with splashes of primary colour, the feint outline of human shapes beginning to form from without the haphazard morass.

"I wanted to go for big bold colours," she told him. "I wanted to both grab the attention and convey a child's sense of helplessness, of being tugged this way and that, of not really knowing what to think and who to believe. Here."

She took his hand again and led him over to a desk strewn with papers, many of them crumpled and flecked with paint.

"Please, take a little while to familiarise yourself with the tone of the rest of the work I've completed so far. I'll go and pop the coffee pot on the stove."

But the more Jacob saw, and the more he understood exactly what Rhea was trying to capture, the more he felt as if she was approaching the whole project from the wrong angle. Everything about what she had done so far was too gimmicky—visually bombastic, full of pop art-esque pretensions, like something a sixth-form college student might do to catch the eye of a lecturer—when, to Jacob's mind, a young person's experiences, from infanthood to their teenage years, were much darker and more complex. Therefore, the use of richer, deeper and more subtle shades would be far more representative, evocative, powerful.

"Erm, Rhea, not to be presumptuous, but I've got a few ideas, reflections from my own childhood, things which might be relevant."

"No, no, not all. I'd love to hear your views, get some feedback." She walked back over with the coffee things on a tray. "That's what's so exciting and rewarding about two artists working together like this."

"Well, when I was a little boy, something happened to me, on the beach, not twenty or so yards from where we sat yesterday morning, something which went on to have a huge impact upon my life."

And he told her about the stone-throwing incident, something he had never told anyone before, he told her about the bigger, older boys, how they had teased him all morning, he told her about that painfully protracted moment when the stone he threw seemed to hang in the air, and how, even to this day, he didn't know if he'd meant to hurt that boy or not, and how it had always troubled him deeply.

"What I think I'm trying to say is that important things happen to us before we really understand what they are, and those things shape us for the rest of our lives. Therefore, your children's attitude toward you may well have been formed long before you and your husband divorced."

Rhea didn't respond, not right away. She scrunched up

her nose, pouted, and wiggled her lips, a gesture Jacob had noticed a lot yesterday, whenever she was mulling things over, when weighing up her words, in the moment between thought and expression.

"So," she said, finally, "you think I should go for even bolder, more intense colours? You think I should—?"

"Not exactly, no," he interrupted—which was a rare thing in itself. "Let me mix up some colours I think would be more appropriate and show you exactly what I mean."

Using a base of yellow and brown, he took up a brush and began to smooth it across the canvas, creating a dense yet swirling effect not unlike the background in Edvard Munch's The Scream. In fact, that very painting may well have been a subconscious influence on Jacob during those early days at Rhea's studio, when the division of artistic labour was truly established, when Rhea did nothing more than stand behind him, looking on, prompting, asking questions just so he would continue what he was doing, or move on to another canvas right away.

"Yes, yes," she enthused. "I see exactly what you mean—those wonderfully rich shades and jerky, almost elliptical strokes really capture a sense of internal conflict. And perhaps we could incorporate that into another piece, one I outlined years ago."

She dashed across the room, grabbing an old sketch and another blank canvas.

"Quick, Jacob, before the brush hardens, work that same effect onto this fresh canvas, will you?"

"Of course, of course," he said, caught up in the moment. "Mix me burnt orange, will you?—only darker, more flavoursome, if that makes sense."

By ten o'clock that evening, having worked for nearly fifteen hours straight, having created an incredible amount of artwork, they collapsed down on Rhea's settee with a bottle of wine.

"What a day!" She laughed and clinked her glass against Jacob's. "Thanks for all your help. You really have been the driving force in bringing my old ideas to fruition."

"Don't mention it," he said. "I'm glad to be of help. In truth, I've rarely worked in such a conducive environment. Not since school have I been anywhere near an area resembling a studio."

Rhea jerked up, turned and faced him.

"Seriously?—an artist of your talent, your passion, your verve. That's criminal, it really is."

Very carefully, she put her wine on the coffee table, stood up, took the band from her hair and shook her tousled locks free.

"Do you know what I like to do after a long day in the studio?" She didn't wait for an answer. "I like to take off all my clothes and just sit here naked, clearing my mind, listening to the far-off sound of the sea."

Without hesitation she did just that, slipping out of her overalls, kicking them away from her ankles.

If looking at her artwork yesterday had been a contrary experience, looking at her naked form was even more beguiling. Never before had Jacob been in the presence of a naked woman. In his younger days, he had, of course, seen the odd pornographic centrefold that was passed from one grubby schoolboy hand to another. On occasion, he had seen nudity on the television, shapely breasts captured in the softest of lights. But Rhea's body, the body of a mother of two, was, to Jacob's eyes, almost too visceral, too real, conjuring visions of Bacon and Lucian Freud. Her breasts were almost shapeless now. Her stomach slack with stretchmarks. The tops of her thighs pitted with cellulite. But it was perhaps the sprawling bush of dark pubic hair between her legs which he found most fascinating. There was simply so much of it; he never knew women could be so abundant in that area. Regardless, she was the most beautiful sight he had ever seen.

Completely unabashed, she took one of the seats at the dining-table, about face, clambering upon it like a rider mounting a horse, and resting her elbows on the back.

"That's better," she said. "I always feel such a sense of freedom when I'm naked. And I would strongly urge you to do the same. Before you do, however, I feel I must put our relations on the proper footing."

Jacob was still too struck by her nakedness to really take in what she was saying, or the ramifications it may have.

"Jacob, I fear having another child so much that I'm afraid full-blown intercourse between us is completely out of the question. It's too painful for me. You understand that, don't you? But you are, of course, free to caress my body, kiss me, hold me. Unfortunately, I cannot touch your member in any way, shape or form, either. For me, the phallus is more dangerous than a whole arsenal of atomic bombs. So, if it pleases you, undress, come to me."

Jacob didn't really know how to take this perplexing revelation. Having never had a woman before, he greatly wanted to make love with Rhea now. Perhaps at the back of his mind, even then, he thought that she might change her mind, eventually, that they would, one day, become passionate lovers. But at this early stage of their relationship, he was happy for them to do no more than hold and caress each other.

Getting to his feet, he peeled off his paint-flecked clothing and walked across the room. Rhea got up and met him halfway. Standing, they shared a warm, tender embrace, an embrace possessed of such intimate affection, Jacob could feel his whole body tremble and tears start to well in his eyes. Drawing him even closer, Rhea hummed a soft, sad tune into his ear and then pressed her lips to his cheek. A delicious mix of emotions very nearly overwhelmed him, because he could never remember anybody holding him in their arms before. And while ignorant of the wonders of lovemaking, the pleasure and intensity of climaxing with a woman, he knew that this kind of closeness to another person would always be enough to sustain him.

"Will—will it always be like this?" he asked, burying his face in her thick dark hair.

"Yes, I promise."

For the next three weeks, Jacob called around to Rhea's living space every morning. With the same application and intensity as the very first night, they completed well over one hundred pieces of artwork together, work of both beauty and power, truly capturing everything Rhea set out to capture—abandonment, confusion, yearning, loss, anger, resentment. Negative energy positively pulsed from Jacob's canvases, creating an almost unnerving visual experience.

"I didn't want to say anything before," she said, as they cleaned their brushes at the end of another hugely productive day, "but an old gallery owner friend of mine got in contact late last week. Nothing's definite, but he might be interested in exhibiting some of my work in London."

"That's fantastic," he said, leaning close and kissing her cheek.

"And I couldn't have done it without you, Jacob. In many ways, this is your work as much as it is mine."

Jacob waved her words away. He wanted no credit for anything he had done. All he yearned for each evening was to drink some good wine and for Rhea to hold him in her arms. Only tonight, something unrelated yet very important troubled his mind.

"And I was thinking," he said, uncertainly, "that tomorrow, I might, erm…bring round some of my own artwork to show you."

Rhea stopped what she was doing, tossed the only partially cleaned brushes aside, and grabbed both his hands.

"Really?" She beamed. "Oh, Jacob, that would be wonderful. I'm thrilled that you trust me that much. It's something I've so been looking forward to."

But the following morning, when Jacob knocked on Rhea's door with his sketchbooks there was no reply. Confused, he exited the building and sat on the bench outside.

Half an hour passed.

Thinking that perhaps she may've been asleep when he knocked previously, he went back inside the building and knocked again. Only this time, he noticed that there was a note lying on the floor, a note with his name on it. Swooping down, he picked it up and opened it.

Dear Jacob,

Had to leave at very short-notice. I didn't have a contact number for you, so I couldn't speak to you direct. I'm so sorry. But my children, they got back in touch with me just after you left last night. They're in London and eager to spend some time with me at last. You, more than anyone else in this world, know what this means to me. I don't know how long I'll be gone. But hope to see you again soon.

Your special friend and collaborator

Rhea

For the next week, Jacob slipped into a dangerously gloomy depression. He received not one single word from Rhea—not that she would've been able to contact him, anyway. Not a day went by when he didn't curse himself for not having had the wherewithal to simply scribble down his address and give it to her at some stage during the last four weeks. It was foolish, a seismic oversight that drove him close to despair.

First thing each morning, he called round to her flat and knocked on the door, but there was never any reply. Crushed, he would walk down to the promenade and sit on the seawall, in the exact same spot he and Rhea had sat on their first date. With bitter longing, he recalled their naked embraces, how tightly she would hold him, how tenderly she pressed her lips to his eyelids then forehead, the soft words of love she would whisper.

He didn't know how he could go on without it.

On the eighth day of her absence, as Jacob passed the newsagent's on the way to knock at her door again, he saw the following on the advertisement board outside: LOCAL ARTIST RHEA HITLON IN MAJOR LONDON EXHIBITION.

Eagerly, he dashed inside and bought himself a copy of the local paper. Flicking to Page Three, he began to devour the text with his eyes:

Local artist, Rhea Hilton, has enjoyed unprecedented success with her first major London exhibition. Ms Hilton, a classically trained artist, was thrilled with the way her powerful work on the theme of parental alienation was received in the capital. 'An artist's life is a very solitary one', she is quoted as saying, 'the hours spent alone in the studio, trying to capture the muse. But without that solitude, without that sense of artistic isolation when, in many ways, the painter is stranded with only their own instincts to guide them, they would never find their own true voice, they would never be able produce such singular pieces of art as I have managed to produce for tonight's exhibition'. In the accompanying photograph, Ms Hilton stands before the most celebrated picture from the whole exhibition, Promise Me No Promises, which is rumoured to have sold for a seven-figure sum.

Jacob lowered the paper.
"Promise me no promises."

5

Death on the Stairs

Jacob Fallada returned home to find his aunt dead in the hallway. From the way her limbs were splayed, from the crooked, unnatural angle of her neck, it was clear that she had taken a violent fall down the stairs. In fact, when Jacob peered up the stairwell, he could clearly see that one of the brass rails and a piece of carpet had come away from a step near the top rung. A freak accident had killed his arch tormentor, a woman who had revelled in his degradation, who had shouted him down at every opportunity, humiliated him in public, abused him with the foulest of language, clouted him around the back of head for the smallest indiscretion. Even if he did something good and worthy, she found heinous fault. For those and many other reasons, Jacob didn't really know how he felt about the situation.

Incredibly calm in the circumstances, he crouched and stared into his dead aunt's face.

"Jesus!" He recoiled, almost stumbled down onto his backside. For her eyes were wide open and possessed of far more warmth, sparkle and kindness in death than they ever possessed in life.

This was something that troubled Jacob the man but intrigued the artist inside him.

When, by rights, he should have been dashing out of the house and informing a local neighbour, or more reasonably, telephoning the emergency services himself, Jacob stepped over his aunt's body, and hurried up to his room for his sketchbook and pencils.

Once back downstairs, he sat before the corpse, cross-legged, and began to sketch the scene, in an attempt to capture exactly what he had seen when he first crouched before her—bright shining eyes in a dead woman's cold blank face.

Tap-tap-tap—knuckles rapped upon the back door.

Jacob gave such a violent start both his pencil and sketchbook went flying up into the air.

A moment later, the back door swung open and heavy footsteps padded across the kitchen floor. Only then did Jacob feel the true weight and enormity of what had happened, and the profound wrongness of what he was then in the midst of doing. Clattering down the hallway came Les Higginbotham, clinically obese man-mountain, owner of around half a dozen chins, long-time widower, a man who, so it was rumoured, had been courting Jacob's aunt for close to two decades.

"What the bloody hell do you think you're doing, boy? What...What's happened to Jeane?"

"I don't know," Jacob replied, clambering up to his feet. "I just got back from a stroll and found her like this."

With tears filling his big brown puffy eyes, Higginbotham looked from the twisted corpse and back to Jacob again.

"Is she...is she...?"

"I'm afraid so," said Jacob, feeling a momentary pang of sympathy, as if Higginbotham was the close relative and Jacob a concerned neighbour breaking the bad news, passing on his condolences.

"Then…Then why didn't you call an ambulance or the police or what have you?" he said, stifling back the sobs. "Why were you sitting on the floor, staring at her like that?" He again looked at the dead body. "And hang on. What's that there?—your bloody sketchbook and pencils. What…? You weren't…weren't drawing her, were you?"

He stared hard at Jacob and took a large, threatening step forward.

"No, no." Jacob backed away, raising both hands, palms upturned. "It's not what it looks like, Mr Higginbotham. I came in with my drawing materials. When I saw her at the bottom of the stairs, her body all bent out of shape, I…I dropped them to the floor."

As if Jacob's words had a ring of legitimacy, Higginbotham stopped what had looked like a murderous advance.

"I don't know about all this," he said, his mounting distress visible in the way he kept shifting his weight and rubbing a hand across his mouth. "You were never on particularly good terms, were you? And she'd been talking 'bout turfing you out for years now."

"I know, I know we had our ups and downs, but we were, erm…close in our own way."

Higginbotham squeezed his eyes shut, took a deep intake of breath and slowly exhaled.

"Close?" He lifted his head. "You were never close."

Much slower than before, but perhaps with a hint of even more menace, Higginbotham took another step closer to Jacob.

"Now wait just a moment, Mr Higginbotham, you're understandably—"

"What's happened?" shouted another neighbour, Gail Proctor, as she rushed into the house. "I saw the back door ajar and heard raised voices."

"It's him," said Higginbotham, jabbing a finger in Jacob's direction. "He's finally offed his poor old aunt."

On seeing the corpse, Gail Proctor brought a hand to her mouth to stifle a scream.

"You...You murdered her, didn't you?" she said breathlessly, after mastering her shock. "You always were an evil little bastard, throwing stones at people down the beach, cracking 'em over the head with golf clubs, pushing young girls into ditches. There was even talk of you raping a woman in the churchyard once. Yeah. Your poor old aunt told me this day would come, told me you were the devil incarnate. 'Gail,' she said, 'mark my words, that bloody nephew of mine, he's devious, underhand, capable of anything. I have to keep my room locked up at night, I do.'"

"That's ridiculous!' cried Jacob. "There aren't even locks on the bedroom doors." He swivelled around and pointed up the stairs. "Go up and have a look if you don't believe me."

"But how'd you explain all this, eh?" said Les. "How come you were sitting there like that? How come you didn't call for help?"

"I told you: I'd only just got back myself."

"I don't believe you." He sniffed and sobbed and made a heavy-handed lunge for the much younger man. "I'll...I'll kill you for this!"

"No!" Gail Proctor leapt in between them. "No, Les, no. We've got to let the police deal with things, we've got to get justice for Jeane."

Somehow, considering the fact she was seventy-six years

old, only five-foot-one, and registered blind, she managed to wrest them away from each other, in the way a sturdy crowbar eases a rusty nail from a piece of wood.

"Calm down, Les," she said. "Mark my words. I won't rest until that arsehole over there is behind bars for the rest of his days."

***

"Okay," said Detective Inspector Hammond, sliding a sketchbook across the table top, "what can you tell us about this, Mr Fallada?"

Jacob picked the sketchbook up and studied the far from finished but far from unimpressive charcoal sketch of his dead aunt.

"I…I don't know," he said, a little disingenuously. It was far simpler than the truth: that he wanted to capture that almost otherworldly moment for posterity. "I…I think I must've been in shock."

Hammond nodded.

"That's understandable." But there was something in his firm, brusque tone which directly contradicted both gesture and words. "But there are a few, erm…shall we say inconsistencies at the scene of your aunt's death."

"Inconsistencies? How do you mean?"

"Well, to all intents and purposes, this looks like a tragic accident, that your aunt had the misfortune of catching her foot on a loose stair rail, falling and breaking her neck. However, our crime scene boys have just got back to me, and it looks as if the rail had been tampered with, quite recently, that perhaps someone deliberately loosened it with malicious intent."

Chilled by the inference, Jacob swallowed hard and shifted in his seat. Never before had he paid the stairs or carpet rail any attention whatsoever. For him, each fifteen steps of the ascent were a means to an end, a way to escape from the horrible atmosphere downstairs to the familiar and welcome calm of his bedroom.

"With that in mind, Mr Fallada, is there anything you'd like to tell us?"

Jacob shook his head.

"You never got on with your aunt, did you? In fact, many of her close friends claim that you were at constant logger-heads, that things often got heated between you, violent, even."

Yes, on her part, Jacob thought with real bitterness, but remained silent on the matter.

"Now, I've been on the force for more than twenty years," said Hammond, "and I've seen it all in my time, even in a quiet little town like this. Back in ninety-eight, we had those cat murders up the Park there. A few years later, we had the case of the councillor who took a shotgun to all and sundry. Only last month, we were called out to that food poisoning case in the next village, chef deliberately infecting custom-ers with deadly bacteria. And do you know the common denominator in all of those cases?"

Jacob shook his head again, even though he sensed the question was showy and rhetorical.

"Up here." Hammond tapped his forehead. "Nut jobs. Loose-bloody-cannons with a chip on their shoulder. Dan-gerous bastards who bore a grudge. And they all had simi-lar backgrounds, were either physically or sexually abused, bullied at school, fostered, never knew their real parents. And I hate to say it, Mr Fallada, but you certainly fit the profile."

There was a long, pregnant pause.

"So, I'll ask you again: is there anything you'd like to tell us about that stair rail? And, remember, if you come clean now, it'll help with your defence; the courts always look favourably upon criminals who confess. It shows sincerity, grave remorse for the evil act perpetrated. And with your background history, you could easily cop a plea. You'd be out in four or five years. So, what'd you say? Are you going to cooperate?"

But Jacob refused to confess to anything, certainly not the murder, or, more correctly, involuntary manslaughter of his aunt through diminished responsibility.

Hammond changed tack. Lowering his voice, and using Jacob's Christian name for the very first time, he said:

"We know she was a tyrant, Jacob. We know she treated you no better than a doormat, that she beat and verbally abused you at every opportunity. We know you haven't got a violent bone in your body, that you suffered at her hands for decades."

He tried to catch Jacob's eyes across the table, but Jacob kept his head lowered, despite feeling the full force of the detective's stare.

"We're on your side, Jacob. Why don't you tell me everything, then we can have a nice cup of tea and get off home, eh?"

But Jacob stood firm.

"No?" Hammond's hopeful look collapsed into an angry, dark, thundery-sky frown. "Okay. On your head be it, son." Abruptly, he pushed his chair back with his legs and got to his feet. "I'm going to go and talk to a few other witnesses now, Mr Fallada, more close friends of your aunt's. In a minute or two, Professor Miriam Ward, a police psychologist, will come and have a chat with you, an informal assessment of your mental state, if you will."

***

"And this teacher," said Professor Ward, looking down at

her notes, "the one who called round to your house when you were seven years old, he told you to never show anybody your artwork?"

"Not exactly," Jacob replied. "He told me that my pictures were 'strange, mature, sophisticated', and that I shouldn't show them to anyone until I understood what they really meant myself."

"Right." Ward frowned and twirled a Biro around in her fingers. "How did you feel about that at the time? And, looking back now, does it not strike you as particularly strange advice?"

Jacob hesitated. He had no real idea how they had come to discuss such matters. As soon as the professor entered the room, she started talking quickly, almost excitedly, about the sketch of his aunt, the one 'found at the scene'. She wanted to know what had compelled him to sit down and draw the corpse, what went through his head as he put pencil to paper; she wanted to know if he considered himself a true artist and, if so, how long he had been drawing for. And he could only tell her the truth on all counts: yes, he did consider himself a true artist and had done so ever since childhood, only he didn't really like to talk about his work all that much, and that he neither knew why he had dedicated his life to such pursuits, or why he sat down in front of his aunt's dead body and started to draw her. 'It's just something I've always done.'

"Erm, not really," Jacob said in answer to her question. "In fact, then as now, it struck me as the best advice I ever received."

This seemed to perplex Ward all over again; she frowned and bit into her bottom lip.

"Okay. Perhaps we're veering off track slightly. Let's return to my original question: why did you start to sketch your aunt's dead body? Why didn't you call the emergency services like any normal, reasonable, conscientious person?"

Having been in custody for over four hours now, Jacob decided to simply tell her the truth, no matter how strange or sinister it made him appear.

"Because when I crouched to look at the body, I saw that my aunt's eyes were wide open and possessed of more kindness, light and love than they ever had when she was alive. And that…and that saddened me because she never seemed capable of the finer feelings, she never seemed a very happy or content person, and for that one moment, I knew, deep down, that if she'd only tried, if circumstances, if her life had been better, if she hadn't have been lumbered with me, perhaps, she might have had a far happier existence."

Nodding enthusiastically, as if every word Jacob had just said made perfect sense, Ward jotted down a series of rapid-fire notes.

"Right, thank you for that, Jacob. You speak very eloquently. Now, I'd like to ask you a couple of things about your past conduct. You haven't got a criminal record, have you? You haven't been in trouble with the police before?"

He shook his head.

"But one or two of your aunt's close friends have suggested that you have been involved in some serious assaults over the years, that you fractured the skull of one boy with a stone, another with a golf club, and that you were guilty of raping a twelve-year-old girl in the town centre, in broad daylight."

Jacob couldn't believe what he was hearing.

"Look," he said, firmly. "In the first incident—or two incidents, I should probably say—they happened within about ten hours of each other—I was seven years old. In the second, or third, I stumbled upon a drunken woman in town. I tried to help. It was a misunderstanding. Hence the fact that the police never made any arrests or pressed any charges."

"Okay. I understand. But why do you think your aunt's friends would bring such matters up at the police station, considering the potential seriousness of the situation? I mean, and not to worry you unduly, but you could well be charged with murder or manslaughter, you could face a significant period in prison. To mention these things to the police now, of all times, seems beyond malicious."

Again, Jacob had to pause to consider an answer. Why had people, throughout his life, taken an instant, almost violent dislike towards him? His appearance? His scruffy hair and dirty clothes? His weakness—both physical and in terms of character? His artistic pretensions? Lifestyle? The fact that the things which motivated, stimulated and justified their existences had never meant anything to him?

"I can only say that this is my fate, that I've always been destined to be shunned by everyday people. And if ever I've tried to do anything about it, to alter my destiny, I've only been shunned all the more. So, I've learnt to accept my lot in life, to withdraw, keep my head down, avoid other people at all costs, and carry on with my artistic work as best I can."

"What?—you mean like in a religious sense, like Job?"

Before Jacob could formulate an answer, two firm knocks sounded against the door.

"Come in," said Professor Ward, half turning in her chair.

"Sorry to interrupt," said a young constable with a crew-cut and eager, punctilious bearing. "But the Guv told me to come and see you straight away. We've just had word from a local repairman. Apparently, Ms Fallada had called him late last week, asking him to fix the loose stair rail. So, erm…we haven't really got any call to hold her nephew any longer."

"Oh, right, I see," said Ward, more than a hint of tangible disappointment in her voice, as if she hoped Jacob would be charged with first-degree murder just so she could carry on talking to him. "Okay, Mr Fallada." She turned back round. "It looks as if you're free to go."

***

When Jacob eventually returned home, he found a white Swinton Reclamations transit-van parked on the road outside. As he opened the garden gate, two great lumbering men in overalls came huffing and puffing out of the front door carrying his aunt's bulky settee.

"Wait!" He ran down the garden path, waving his hands above his head. "What are you doing? You can't just remove all my aunt's furniture. She's only just died, for pity's sake?"

"Not our problem, son," said one of the red-faced beef-cakes. "We're just, ah…doing our job. Go and have a word with my boss. He's in one of the upstairs bedrooms, 'bout to throw out a load of old junk, papers, sketchbooks, and what have you."

"What?"

Jacob squeezed his way around the removal men, pushed his way into the house, past the spot where his dead aunt had lain not more than six or seven hours ago, and raced up the stairs, stumbling, ironically, on the loose rail which had caused her untimely death.

"What do you think you're doing?" he cried, on seeing a round-faced man in an ill-fitting suit tossing his treasured artwork into white hessian sacks with the words: *For Immediate Incineration* printed on the sides.

He stopped what he was doing and looked up from his clipboard.

"Are you the nephew? The other householder?"

"Yes, that's right. And these are my personal belongings, my artwork, years of creative toil."

"Is it?" He pulled a pouty, unconvinced face and hunched his shoulders. "I'm sorry, my man. Take whatever you want, 'cause believe me, there's nothing in this room that's of any worth whatsoever."

Jacob felt close to refuting the point, and in the strongest possible terms—because there are some things in this life that you simply can't put a monetary value to—but he sensed there was something desperate about this situation, and if he didn't seek an immediate resolution, it might be too late.

"But what are you doing?" he asked, while rescuing his artwork from the sacks of death.

"Removing all and sundry items of value. This property and everything in it is rightly ours now."

"What? No. There must be some mistake. This is my aunt's house. She literally died, having taken a nasty fall down the stairs, a handful of hours ago."

"And you have my sincerest condolences, but there's been no mistake—we don't make mistakes." Briefly, he returned to his clipboard. "Jeane Fallada, right? Three Carrington Road, right?"

Jacob nodded, even though he still didn't understand.

"She was into some big firm for a lot of money—club books, Littlewoods, the usual suspects. The upshot of which means, she lost the house, she lost everything. If she hadn't have taken a tumble, we'd have been round sooner rather than later."

Jacob took a moment to process this information.

"You mean I haven't got anywhere to live anymore? You mean I can't stay here tonight, like normal?"

"Well, you'll probably be all right for tonight, son—maybe tomorrow. Who knows? Minus any furniture, of course. But best you get yourself down to the solicitor's first thing. Here." He rummaged around in his pocket and pulled out a standard business card. "That's the name of the people you need to speak to."

***

"That's the thing, Mr Fallada," said Leslie Priest of Priest, Jenkins and Co. Solicitors. "As your aunt was in such serious financial difficulties, the firm you saw yesterday were well within their rights to clear the property forthwith."

"But she'd only been dead a few hours. How on earth is that legal? Surely they have to wait a certain period of time before they just march in and take everything."

"I'm afraid not. This is the modern world. Things move fast. If the firm working on behalf of her main creditor didn't act in a swift and decisive manner, then an agent from one of the more minor firms would undoubtedly have done so. Either way, the house would've been stripped bare in a matter of hours. We, in the legal profession, call it the piranha effect."

"Piranha effect?"

"Yes, a rather apt image, wouldn't you say? As the gregarious predatory freshwater fish of the genus Serrasalmus is able to strip the flesh from a human bone in a matter of seconds." He chuckled, as if to himself. "There is, however, some small provision for you in your aunt's last will and testament."

"Really?"

"Yes, of course," said Priest, as if Jacob's aunt was possessed of saint-like qualities of kindness and generosity. "You were blood, after all. And after all the travails of your early life, she always had great affection for you."

Jacob found this even harder to believe but sensed the futility and inappropriateness of expressing the fact at the present moment.

"So, you'll be glad to learn that you aren't going to be out on the streets. Your aunt made sure that you'd always have a roof over your head, long-term accommodation, as it were, by way of permanent access to the family's old mobile home down Black Crow's Lane."

"But that's…that's in the fishing village up the road, that's in the middle of nowhere. And it isn't a mobile home but my great-uncle's caravan."

Mr Priest shrugged and threw up his hands.

"At least it's something, eh, Mr Fallada? Here." He pushed a set of rusty keys across the desktop. "At least you won't be out on the streets. At least it's somewhere you can call your own."

***

It took Jacob well over twenty minutes to navigate his way down the narrow, rutted dirt-track overgrown with thick bramble bushes and all kinds of stubborn vegetation. More than once, he had to put down his meagre possessions and take a few deep intakes of breath before resuming his trek to what Mr Priest had called "somewhere of his own".

When he finally got to the bottom of the track, Jacob couldn't quite believe what he saw. In a secluded clearing, in the shadow of several grand old oak trees, stood a dilapidated, mildewed caravan, missing its wheels, with one window boarded-up, and a rusted old aerial dangling from the roof.

Still breathing heavily, he put his bags down again and looked right and left. Closing his eyes, he listened to something that wasn't quite silence—there was a gentle breeze rustling through the trees, the odd soothing, chirruping birdsong, maybe even the far-off sounds of waves breaking on the shoreline—but something that was as close to silence as Jacob Fallada had ever known before.

"Home at last."

6

Three Little Boys

Jacob Fallada heard the boys long before he saw them. Their shrill, panicky voices carried all the way down the deserted dirt-track leading to the dilapidated caravan he now called home. Jacob was unused to such interruptions. He rarely interacted with other people. The nearest dwelling was several miles away. If he required any provisions, he had to hike across fields and through woodland to a remote village shop. At this time of year, the entrance to the dirt-track was overgrown, concealed from the road, the surface itself boggy and rutted with potholes, almost impassable. How the boys had stumbled upon it, let alone made it all the way down to the bottom end, was baffling, an impossibility almost. For this reason, Jacob abandoned his artistic work, pulled on a thick winter coat, and went outside to investigate.

Since early morning, patchy mist had been rolling in off the sea, enveloping the surrounding countryside in a wispy, shifting curtain of gloom. Through this curtain appeared three sturdy looking young boys in waterproof clothing, scarves, bobble-hats, and wellington-boots.

"Look," said one, pointing at Jacob. "A man. He's sure to be able to help."

"What's the matter? What's happened? How come you're out here, in the middle of nowhere, all on your own?"

"We were with our fathers," said the same boy as before, "on a daytrip to the seaside, a nature walk. They went down to the shoreline to see if it was safe for us to walk along the beach. They told us to wait near the shelter by the slip-way. But they never came back."

Jacob listened to all of this with a mounting sense of unease, scrutinising each boy in turn, studying them at closer quarters, for they were the mirror-image of the three boys who had tormented him at school, who had teased, beat and humiliated him in front of the other children.

"What are your names?" he felt compelled to ask.

"That's Shane. That's Will. And I'm Zac."

Jacob shuddered. Shane, Will and Zac had been the names of his tormentors. Not only did the boys now standing in front of him bear an uncanny resemblance to the bullies of yesteryear, but they had the exact same names.

"We're scared," said Shane, the slightly bigger, bulkier of the three children. "We want to find our dads. We want to go home."

"I…I understand," said Jacob, mastering his emotions, telling himself that this was no more than a bizarre coincidence, that his memory was playing tricks on him, that the boys didn't resemble the Shane, Will and Zac of the past as closely as he had originally thought. "So, you were told to wait by the shelter near the slip-way leading down to the beach, right? Only your fathers didn't return. You went out to search for them and couldn't find your way back again?"

Each boy nodded earnestly.

"Okay. Perhaps it would be best if we retraced your steps, then. I'm sure your fathers lost their way in the mist. I'm sure we'll find them without too much trouble."

But Jacob knew how treacherous that stretch of coastline could be in these conditions. In the past, he had heard stories of ramblers or birdwatchers going missing when venturing along the shore, never to be seen again.

"Follow me."

They walked along the dirt-track, ducking to avoid overhanging bramble bushes, squelching through thick mud, stepping over rutted potholes full of dull, brownish water. Every twenty or so paces, Jacob would steal a glance at one of the boys. Each time, a painful memory rose to the forefront of his mind. He remembered the day Zac pinned him down and made him eat pieces of mouldy orange peel. He remembered the time Will had accosted him in the sports hall changing-rooms, stripped him naked and pushed him out into the corridor, so all the other children saw him naked. Or the time Shane slashed his forearms with a protractor, slicing his skin, drawing blood time and again. But what haunted him most of all, as they turned and made their way down towards the main coast road, were memories of those horrible bullies laughing at him, how much pleasure they derived from inflicting the utmost pain.

"Did you come this way?" Jacob asked them.

"I don't think so," said Will. "I'm sure we came over a railway bridge."

"I see." This baffled Jacob all the more. The nearest railway bridge was several miles away. If they had come from that direction, then they must have been walking for hours before they stumbled upon his caravan. "Right, we better cross over."

They crossed the main road, and walked down a narrow, winding lane that led all the way up to the cliff tops.

"Right," said Jacob, bringing them to a halt. "The lane up ahead is always flooded. To get past, we'll have to walk along the grass bank. You must be very careful, though. The ground is saturated, treacherous, very slippery. If you don't display sufficient caution you could fall into the boggy pit in the field to your left. So perhaps it would be best if I walked behind you."

"But what if the boy at the front lost his footing and fell?" asked Will. "You'd be too far away to help."

"You're right," said Jacob. "Maybe I should be in the middle, then."

"But there are four of us," said Shane. "How can you be in the middle? Four, after all, is an even number."

"Of course it is," said Jacob. "What I meant to say is: one of you will lead the way. I will follow directly behind. The other two boys will bring up the rear, as it were."

"But why not have two at the front and one behind?" said Zac. "Surely that would make more sense. We're walking forwards not backwards. If we get into any difficulties it would be much easier to help a boy in front of you rather than behind, wouldn't it?"

"Okay, okay," said Jacob, losing patience at this point. "We can't stand here all day arguing. Zac, you go first. Will, you next. I will be directly behind you. Shane will be directly behind me."

This decided, they clambered up onto the bank and proceeded to edge very slowly, very carefully along the soft muddy grass. Halfway down, despite the caution displayed, Zac slipped over onto his backside, arms flailing.

"Ah!" he cried out.

Lunging forward, Jacob grabbed hold of his wrist, stopping him from sliding off the bank. Startled, Shane lost his footing completely, and went tumbling from the verge, crashing through the adjoining bushes, plopping into the bog below.

"Help!" he shouted, splashing around in the thick quagmire. "Help!"

Jacob scrambled along the bank on all fours. "Shane! Shane!" But there was no response.

"Where is he?" asked Will. "Where's he gone?"

Jacob called out time and again. But still there was no answer. Crouching closer, he stretched out a hand, searching for the boy's body, but all he encountered was the boggy ground, the clingy, cloying feel of cold, sticky mud.

"I'm going to have to wade in." He lowered his legs into the quagmire, inching deeper into the mud, trying to find the bottom. "It's very deep. But I might just be able to get some kind of foothold."

The mist was much thicker now; he could barely see a hand in front of him as he waded through mud up to his waist, doing a complete sweep of the surrounding area. But it was all in vain; Shane was nowhere to be seen.

After ten minutes of fruitless searching, Jacob hauled himself up out of the bog.

"I...I can't find him," he said, struggling to keep the tears from his voice. "He must've got dragged under, he must've..."

"How could this have happened?" said Zac.

"It was an accident," Jacob replied, struck by the boy's harsh, accusatory tone.

"But you're an adult," he went angrily on. "By offering to help us find our fathers, you took responsibility for our welfare. If one of us gets hurt or lost or whatever, then it's down to you to put it right. You've got to try again. You've got to wade through the mud until you find him."

"Impossible," said Jacob. "It's too thick. If I risked another foray into the swamp, I may well be dragged under, too."

"Then you must hand yourself into the police."

"The police? Why?"

"Because you've failed in your duty of care towards us."

"It's not my fault," Jacob argued. "I took you aside, back there, not fifteen minutes ago, and warned you of the dangers. I told you to watch your footing. I told you how slippery the grass would be."

"What are we going to do?" cried Will. "What are we going to do?"

"Calm down," said Jacob. "Look. We've made it this far. If we use the cliff tops to guide us down to towards the beach, we might just be able to get to the shelter. We might just be able to find your fathers. Agreed?"

The boys reluctantly nodded their heads.

"Come on. Follow me."

On higher ground the wind was much stronger, the mist thicker still. To be extra safe, Jacob insisted that they hold hands as they walked along the undulating terrain, keeping to the grassy knolls, being careful to avoid the very edge of the cliffs.

"How much further?" asked Zac, coming to a stop, letting go of Jacob and Will's hands.

Jacob surveyed the blank, blustery scene.

"Not far now," he replied. "If my calculations are correct, the shelter should be just down this incline. There's a car park of sorts, a concreted area. Once we reach there, the shelter is only a stone's throw away."

"What's that?" asked Will.

Both Jacob and Zac swung round. Will had wandered over to the edge of the cliff, and was now pointing at something which had caught his attention.

"No!" shouted Jacob, darting out a hand to drag him away from danger. But he missed completely. Will tottered, swayed, and toppled into the misty abyss. "Will!" Jacob scrambled down on his knees, close to the ledge, staring into nothing more than a blank void.

"No!" he repeated despairingly. He couldn't believe what was happening. An hour ago, he had been absorbed in his artistic work, thinking of nothing more than expressing himself to the full. Now two young boys had lost their lives within a quarter of an hour of each other. He sniffed and rubbed his eyes. He looked at the exact spot where Will had fallen. All that was left, caught in the tangled coastal scrub, was one of his wellington-boots.

Zac started to cry.

"Don't, please," said Jacob, getting to his feet. "He…He shouldn't have wandered off like that. He knew we were walking close to the edge of the cliffs. He knew it was dangerous. I only let go of his hand for a second—a second. If anything, it was you who stopped. I—"

"I want to go home," Zac sobbed. "I want my dad."

"Yes, yes, of course you do." He took the boy's hand. "The shelter is just down here. Come on."

They set off once again. The waves crashing on the shore below frothed and fizzed, the stiff blustery wind buffeted them all way down to the car parking area, where the mist started to thin. Up ahead, Jacob could just about see the outline of a wooden structure.

"Look," he said, pointing. "There's the shelter."

They raced over but found it empty. Jacob walked from front to back. Nothing. No sign of anyone at all.

"There doesn't seem to be anyone here," he said, slumping down on the bench inside. "What do you want me to do?—walk down the slip-way, walk along the beach, call out, see if I can find your father?"

But Zac just stood there, directly in front of Jacob, head lowered, his hands thrust deep into his pockets.

"Zac? I said, what do you want me to do?"

In time, he lifted his head. "You did that on purpose, didn't you?"

"What?"

"I didn't see what happened to Shane—not really. I'd slipped over. I was scared, busy trying to hold onto the bank, to stop myself from falling. But with Will, I saw you push him off the cliff."

"What? No!" cried Jacob. "What are you saying? I rushed over to help. I didn't get there in time. It was a complete accident. I—"

"Two accidents in such a short space of time," said Zac, very calmly now. "I don't believe you. I think you only led us down such a treacherous route so you could kill us."

"Kill you! Why would I want to kill you? I was hard at work when you came shouting and screaming down the track. As I rule, I never leave a piece of artistic work unfinished. All I've tried to do is help."

"Some help! Just you wait. When our fathers return, they're sure to want answers. I'll tell them that I saw you push Will over the cliff top. I'll tell them everything: how Shane suddenly disappeared like that, that one minute he was calling out for help, the next, you'd leapt off the bank, that in all likelihood you drowned him in that muddy bog."

"Wait just a minute!"

As Jacob stood up, Zac charged forward, beating him about the head and chest with his balled fists, forcing him back down to the bench. Unprepared for such a vicious and determined assault, Jacob took a few significant blows to the face, making his eyes flood with water. Blindly, he raised his hands, trying to defend himself. In this manner, they grappled, struggled, fell wrestling to the ground, breathless, rolling from side to side. Gradually, Jacob's superior strength overwhelmed the boy. He clambered on top of him and put his hands around his throat. As Zac gasped and gurgled and kicked out his legs, Jacob squeezed as hard as he could, until the thrashing desperate movements subsided, until the boy's body went limp.

Slowly Jacob came to his senses, finding himself staring into Zac's lifeless eyes. He had killed him outright. He had strangled him with his bare hands.

Approaching voices roused him back into the here and now. Thinking fast, he picked up the boy's crumpled body, carried it around to the back of the shelter and dumped it in a drainage ditch, pushing the corpse down below the surface with the toe of his boot, until it was completely submerged.

When he returned, three well-built men in waterproof clothing were standing in the shelter, stamping their feet and rubbing their hands together, trying to warm themselves up.

"Look." One of them pointed at Jacob. "A chap's just appeared out of nowhere, a local chap, no doubt, he's sure to be able to help."

"What's happened?" said Jacob, struggling to mask his distress. "How come you're out here, in the middle of nowhere, all on your own?"

"We could ask you the same question," said the bigger, bulkier of the three men. "It's not a day to be out for a stroll, is it? What are you doing here?"

"Me? I'm...I'm an artist. I was just out walking, trying to absorb myself in the scenery, trying to get some, erm...

inspiration from nature."

"An artist, you say?"

Jacob nodded his head. "What about you?"

"We're on a daytrip with our sons, a nature walk. We didn't realise the weather was going to be this bad. We wanted to check that it was safe to walk along the beach. We asked the boys to stay here. But we got lost. When we returned, they were gone. Have you seen them, three-nine-year-olds wrapped up in hats and scarves?"

Jacob listened to all of this with a mounting sense of unease, scrutinising each man in turn, studying their familiar features at closer quarters. For these men were grown-up versions of the three boys who had tormented him at school.

"No," he lied with surprising conviction. "I haven't seen anyone."

"Shit," said Will senior. "Where the hell could they have got to?"

"You are a local man, though, aren't you?" Zac senior asked Jacob, stepping forward of his companions. "Could you help us search for our boys?"

"Erm, yes, I am local, and I'd be more than happy to help."

Taking it in turns, the three men asked Jacob various questions about the likely route the three boys would have taken, and how far they could have ventured. Even though he was still reeling inside, Jacob offered useful pointers and advice; he managed to master not only his fear but a growing sense of irritation, because these men clearly didn't recognise him from their school days. After all they had put him through, the tears, humiliation, the sleepless nights he endured, still he was a complete nobody to them.

"So, you think it's best if we walk along the cliff tops,

then?" asked Shane senior.

"Yes," he replied, honestly. As much as he didn't want to retrace his steps, there literally was no other way up to the main road.

"Okay," said Will senior. "We'll let you lead the way."

As they set off, Zac senior made a grab for Jacob's elbow.

"Wait. What's that in your pocket?"

Jacob reached inside his pocket, pulling out a length of woollen material. He looked at his right hand as if it was somebody else's. Scrunched up in his palm was Zac's scarf.

"Oh this, I, erm…found it on the cliff tops, just up there." He let the scarf fall to the ground.

Swooping down, Zac senior picked it up. In that one moment, as he crouched with the back of his head exposed, completely unknowing and defenseless, Jacob felt a dark, uncharacteristic impulse to strike him, to punish him for all the bad things he had done in the past.

"Well, if he lost his scarf up there," he said, staring at the cliff tops, oblivious to the violent thoughts flashing through Jacob's mind, "they no doubt headed up towards the main coast road."

"Must've done," said Will senior. He turned to Jacob. "Come on. Show us the way."

"Erm, yes, of course." He darted a nervous look over his shoulder, in the direction of the ditch behind the shelter, but none of the other men seemed to notice. "Follow me."

As they picked their way along the sloping, uneven ground, struggling through long rustling grass, Will senior let out a cry and dashed over to the edge of the cliff.

"Look," he shouted over his shoulder. "There's a welling-ton-boot here, on the ledge."

Inwardly, Jacob cursed himself. As best he could, he had tried to lead them away from the spot where Will junior had plunged to his death.

"You don't think they've fallen over the edge, do you?" his father turned and asked Jacob.

"No, no," he replied, feeling a second mad, dark urge towards violence, towards pushing this man over the cliff, to send him tumbling to his death, to kill him, to right so many past wrongs.

"I don't like it," said Will senior, addressing his two friends. "But it's not like we can go and investigate now, is it? We'd never get down there; the tide's all the way in. We've no other option than to get up to the main road, maybe hail down a passing car or lorry."

"That may present us with a few problems," said Jacob. "The track leading down from the main road is flooded. And even if we manage to circumnavigate it, traffic rarely passes through these parts on days like this."

"Never mind," said Shane senior. "We'll just have to climb up onto the bank and walk around the standing water. The boys have been gone for hours now. We've got to at least give it a try."

When they got to the lane, they clambered up onto the grass bank, and slowly trudged through the soft, saturated grass. About halfway along, Shane senior spotted something caught in one of the bare tangled bushes.

"Hey," he said, pivoting to the side, arms outstretched, almost losing his balance. "It's Shane's bobble-hat. I'm sure of it." He went down on one knee, leaned forward, and tugged the hat from the bush, freeing it up.

As he examined it in his hands, Jacob sidled up alongside him. Vividly, he recalled the extremities of the swamp-like bog, the time he spent frantically searching for this man's son, how, on more than one occasion, he nearly got pulled under by the overwhelming weight of all that mud.

He knew how difficult it would be for anyone not expecting to fall in to haul themselves out again, that, with one firm push, he could condemn Shane senior to a horrible death, the kind of death a horrible bastard like him truly deserved.

"This is bad," said Zac senior. "Look at the thick pools of mud in the field there. If one of our boys slipped and fell, I don't think they'd stand a chance of dragging themselves out again."

"Granted," said Will senior. "But we've got to remain positive. Just because we've found a few items of clothing, doesn't necessarily prove that something terrible has happened. I mean, what are the chances of all of them meeting a bad end, within a few hundred yards of each other?"

"Exactly," said Shane senior. "And boys their age are always losing stuff, aren't they?" He turned to Jacob. "Do you live close by? Have you got a phone?"

"Yes. I live five or so minutes away in, erm…temporary accommodation, a caravan just up the road, the only dwelling for miles around. But I'm afraid I haven't got a telephone or any internet access or anything like that. By choice, I might add. My artistic work is very important to me. I abhor interruptions of any kind."

"Never mind all that." Shane senior took a mobile phone from his jacket pocket. "Damn! Still can't get a signal. Maybe, on higher ground, maybe back at this chap's humble abode, we might be able to contact the emergency services. Agreed?"

"Agreed," his two friends said at one and the same time.

"Besides, we need to warm up. I take it you've got electricity? A kettle? I take it you can make us a cup of tea?"

"Yes. Yes, of course. And, like you say, maybe you can get a phone signal a little further inland. And, who knows, maybe your boys have stumbled upon my homestead, maybe they're there now."

They made their way up the winding lane, crossed the main road, and walked in the direction of Jacob's caravan. Every twenty or so paces, he would steal a glance at one of the men. Each time, he remembered the critical moments that had just passed, when he had the chance to strike out at them. He remembered the back of Zac's head, so inviting. He remembered Will kneeling close to the edge of the cliff, and Shane leaning over that quagmire of mud. If only he had been brave enough to grasp the opportunity, he might have been able to exorcise some painful demons, once and for all.

"Is that it?" said Zac, pointing at the rundown, mildewed caravan with boarded-up windows. "You actually live in a piece of shit like that?"

"Erm, yes," Jacob replied, wincing at Zac's mocking tones, reminiscent of all the times their younger incarnations had terrorised him. "I know it's not much, but it serves my artistic needs well."

Both Shane and Will were busy checking their mobile phones.

"Any joy?" asked Zac.

Will lifted his head. "No, nothing. It's like being in a third world country out here."

"Me neither." Shane clicked his phone shut. "But I could certainly do with a hot drink." He turned to Jacob. "Put the kettle on, will you?"

"Of course, of course," he gabbled in reply. "Please, come inside, take off your coats, try and dry off."

Once inside, Jacob rushed over to the far end of the caravan and drew a thin curtain across his desk, the quiet nook where he worked so intently each day.

"I'd, erm…rather not show you any of my artistic work,"

he said, in all seriousness. He hated the idea of being ridiculed by these three men, these enemies, his former tormentors.

"As you wish," said Zac, stepping to the side, making room for his two friends.

"Please, sit down, over there." Jacob pointed to a tatty and torn banquette. "There's not much space, I'm afraid. But at least it's warm and dry, eh?"

He then went over to the sink and filled the kettle from a wonky, rusted faucet.

"Is tea okay for you?" he asked, flicking the switch.

"Fine, fine," said Will. "But do you really think the boys could find their way here? Not to question your judgment, but the dirt-track is almost completely obscured from the road. The surface itself is boggy and potted with holes. I have grave doubts as to whether boys their age would be able to get all the way down to the bottom end."

"Agreed," said Zac. "And the fact we can't pick up a signal here means this whole excursion has been a terrible waste of time. Our boys are out there somewhere, freezing-cold, scared."

"You're right," said Shane. "We shouldn't have come here. We should've kept searching. We should've waited at the side of the road for a passing vehicle, someone who could've gone to the local police station, who could've informed the coastguard."

Cringing inside, Jacob listened to them shout and curse. To be in such close proximity to these men again, to see hands which had once clasped his throat, fists which had once pummelled his face, feet which had once kicked out and stamped on his body, appalled him.

"How far is the nearest town from here?" Shane got to his feet and walked across the creaky-floored caravan.

"How far is…?" he trailed off. "Hang on." He picked an old letter up off the dining-table and studied it closely. "Is your name Jacob Fallada?"

Jacob lowered his eyes and swallowed hard.

"What?" said Zac, standing also. "*The* Jacob Fallada, our Jacob Fallada, the little pipsqueak from school, the smelly bastard, the freak who was always pissing in his pants?"

"Ha!" Will shot to his feet and clapped his hands together. "I thought there was something familiar about you."

All three edged into the kitchen area, rounding on Jacob in the exact same way they had rounded on him at school.

"Well, Jacob," said Shane, making a sweeping gesture, taking in the whole caravan, "you've certainly done well for yourself. Ha! Look at this luxury palace. Then again, you always were the most likely to succeed, weren't you?"

The other two snorted with laughter.

"So, this is what you've been doing with yourself all these years? Christ! Will you take a look at this place, boys? Fallada is like a rat in his own personal sewer."

Jacob just stood there with his head lowered, concentrating on the low rumble of the kettle, willing it to boil, willing them to leave him alone, to finally be out of his head.

"Remember that time you ate all that mouldy orange peel?" asked Zac, winking at his friends. "Always been a man of refined tastes."

"Or that time you exposed yourself outside the sports hall changing-rooms," said Will. "Always were a filthy little pervert, weren't you, Fallada, eh?"

"Or when he cut himself with that protractor," said Shane. "Bloody attention seeker. Can't say it surprises me: shit living in shit."

"You were such a pathetic specimen," said Zac. "And what? You call yourself an artist now, do you? Bloody vagrant, more like. Where's this artistic work, anyway? Over there, behind the curtain, in the corner? Best I have a little look; best I run a critical eye over it, eh?"

"No, no," said Jacob, stepping in front of him. "Really, I must insist. I—"

"What?" shouted Zac. "Are you going to try and stop me?" He jabbed a finger into Jacob's chest. "Are you going to raise your hands to me?"

Jacob took a few short, sharp breaths. "I'm…I'm glad I hurt them," he blurted out. "I'm glad they're dead. I'm glad they won't have the chance to grow up to be evil bastards like you."

"What?" cried Shane, pushing past Zac. "What are you talking about? Our boys? I swear, Fallada, if you've laid one finger on them I'll kill—" shrill, panicky voices sounded from outside.

"What's that?" said Zac, swinging round.

"That must be them," said Will. "Old piss pants Fallada was right, after all. They found their way here."

In complete disbelief, Jacob pushed his way past the others, threw open the door, and rushed out of the caravan.

Through another thick curtain of mist appeared the three little boys.

"Look," said Zac junior, pointing at Jacob. "There he is."

Jacob stepped forward, open-armed, relieved that his ordeal was over, that all the murderous nastiness of before had been nothing but a crazy delusion, that he hadn't hurt the boys in any way

"Don't worry," he said. "Your fathers are in the caravan. They're having a nice cup of tea. Everything's going to be all right."

"Our fathers?" said Shane, pulling a shiny protractor out of his jacket pocket. "We haven't come here to find our fathers, Fallada. We've come here for you."

7

The Jacqueline Prophecies

Jacob Fallada didn't know what shocked him more: that a hulking St Bernard was sitting on a stool at the bar, smoking a cigar, or that nobody else in the traditional hostelry was paying the immense canine any attention—not the morose-looking old-timers sitting at a nearby table, or the much younger, smartly dressed couple deep in conversation in a booth by the window.

Almost involuntarily, Jacob found himself walking towards the bar. When he reached the counter, he stole a quick glance at the dog. Its thick white coat had black and brownish flecks; its bull-like neck—its whole body seemed to ripple with a heaving, muscular vitality that was as impressive as it was intimidating.

The barman, a shifty, wall-eyed Transcaucasian, shuffled over.

"What can I get you?" he asked Jacob.

There was a brief silence, where Jacob tried to divert the barman's attention, discretely nodding in the direction of the dog, his eyes (if the barman had been observant enough to notice) clearly said: *Look, there's a huge dog at the end of the bar, smoking a cigar, don't you think that's a little strange?* But there was nothing, not a glimmer of recognition, indicating that the barman did indeed find the St Bernard's presence in any way unusual.

"I said: what can I get you?"

"Oh, sorry, miles away," Jacob lied. "I'll have, erm…one of those, please." He pointed to one of the real ales; one of the cheapest drinks available.

"Coming right up."

As the barman pulled off the pint, Jacob darted another glance at the St Bernard, happily smoking away, seemingly oblivious to everything, like any thoughtful, melancholy drinker found in any bar across the globe.

"There you go." The barman put Jacob's dark, frothy pint on the counter. "That'll be seven-forty, please."

"Right, okay." As he took a handful of coins out of his pocket, Jacob felt duty-bound to make some reference to the dog. "I, erm…didn't know smoking was allowed in public places anymore."

Something he immediately regretted. For the dog shifted its immense body around on the stool, and glared at him.

"No, no," said the barman, "that only applies to humans—the smoking ban, I mean. Far as the management is concerned, any of our canine regulars are more than welcome to enjoy a smoke at the bar."

"Oh, right, that sounds reasonable enough," said Jacob, nervously, feeling the weight of the dog's stare. "Not that it bothers me in the slightest. I happen to love the smell of a good cigar. It's just that I wasn't aware of the regulations." He placed a final coin on the counter. "There you go. Thanks very much."

The barman gathered up the coins and walked over to the cash register.

As Jacob reached for his ale, the canine started speaking to him in a clear human voice.

"You have a problem with me smoking at the bar, young man?"

"Erm, no, no, not all." Jacob put his glass back on the counter. "I was, if anything, just conversation-making with the barkeep. I meant no offence, believe me."

"Oh, I see, just conversation-making."

"That's right."

The dog looked Jacob up and down, as if appraising his appearance—worn-out plimsolls, frayed jeans, a thin T-shirt held together with safety pins, and a scruffy mop of hair—as much as his character.

"You don't come here very often, do you?"

"No, no," Jacob replied. "In my younger days, I used to love public houses, but everything has become so expensive these days, and my artistic work doesn't pay very well. In fact, it barely covers my rent and living expenses, so luxuries like this"—he gestured towards his drink—"are few and far between."

"And what's your name?"

"Jacob, Jacob Fallada."

"Hans," said the dog, offering Jacob a paw to shake. "Pleasure to meet you. And you're an artist, you say?"

"That's correct. Although I don't like to talk about my work all that much."

"I understand," said Hans, exhaling a cloud of billowy smoke out of the side of his jaws. "You artistic types can be very temperamental. Besides, characters like you and I don't come to places like this to talk about our lives and work. We come to escape from all of that, if only for an hour or two. No?"

"Exactly," said Jacob. "Sometimes it's good to get away from things."

"That it is," said Hans. "And are you married, Jacob Fallada? You have children? You are a family man?"

"No, no. Unfortunately, I've not been blessed with the best of luck when it comes to women. And in a small town like this it's hard to meet new people."

"You must get lonely at times, though?"

Jacob shifted uncomfortably. "Erm, yes, of course I do, every now and then. But my work is very time-consuming, it requires a huge amount of dedication, is a very solitary occupation, you might say."

"But you must miss having a woman close, no?"

"Well…" Jacob could feel his cheeks redden.

"It's all right, Jacob. I didn't mean to embarrass you. It's just that I have a friend, a young lady who's not had the best of luck in the romance stakes of late herself, a young lady who might be of interest to you. Perhaps I should give her a call. Perhaps she'll come here this evening to meet you."

Jacob started to protest. "Oh no, don't go to any trouble. I have very little by way of money at the moment, a relationship, even a quiet drink in company, therefore, is beyond my means. So please, I—"

Hans raised a paw, gesturing for quiet. "Jacob. Listen to me. Have you ever heard the expression 'the heart of a dog'?"

"Erm, no, I don't think so. Although I must say, I've always much preferred dogs to cats. Cats, to my mind, have little substance or loyalty and—"

"Jacob," Hans interrupted once again, "please don't digress. What I'm trying to say is that I will call my friend. If she's available, and willing to come and meet you tonight, I'm more than happy to buy you a bottle of wine."

"Oh, no. I don't think I'd feel comfortable doing that. I've only just met you. It wouldn't be right. Besides, why would you do such a thing?"

Hans let out a friendly, good-natured chuckle. "Call me a silly romantic, a matchmaker, but as soon as I saw you walk through that door"—Hans gestured towards the main entrance—"I sensed a deep unhappiness in you, that perhaps your life wasn't going all that well. And clearly, despite your age—late twenties, early thirties, I'm guessing—you have little experience with women and little confidence in yourself."

"Oh, I wouldn't say that," said Jacob. "It's just that, as I said before, I've dedicated myself to my artistic work, and have had very little time for women, for socialising in general."

"All the more reason for me to contact"—Hans hesitated, and for the first time he looked unsure of himself—"let's call her Jacqueline for the time being. That, of course, is not her real name, but at this early stage it would probably be best if you referred to her by a false name, to provide a level of anonymity that I'm sure would make her feel much more comfortable."

"But you make it sound so businesslike, so cold. In the past, if I met a woman, we would never think of concealing our true names, and our relations, if we liked each other's company, would develop naturally."

"Jacob, Jacob, Jacob, you really have been existing in some kind of social void for far too long. Things have changed. People do things much differently these days." Hans took another draw on his cigar and exhaled another cloud of smoke. "Now, do you want me to contact Jacqueline or not? It's entirely up to you." He looked at the clock on the wall behind the bar near the optics. "It's still early, not quite seven o'clock yet. Plenty of time for the two of you to enjoy a pleasant evening together."

***

"Ah, here she is." Hans ushered a tall, incredibly pretty young woman over to the bar. "This is Jacob Fallada, the prospective suitor I told you about over the telephone."

Their eyes met; both quickly looked away.

"For tonight, we've decided to call you Jacqueline. I hope that's all right. I just felt, in light of recent events, that it would be better to keep a level of personal anonymity. If you want to tell Jacob your real name later, that is, of course, entirely up to you."

As Hans talked, Jacob looked Jacqueline over. Clearly nervous, unsure of herself, she had shiny auburn hair cut into a fringe, pale skin, prominent cheekbones, and was heavily made-up around the eyes and mouth. She wore a long armless, halter-neck blouse that showed off the many colourful tattoos running up and down her arms, all depicting human faces.

"Nice to meet you, Jacob." They shook hands.

"And you," he said, with a composure that surprised himself. "You look very lovely tonight."

"Thank you." Once again their eyes met, and once again, they both quickly looked away. "That's very sweet of you to say."

Hans coughed, cleared his throat, and pointed across the barroom.

"There on the table in the corner, the one with the candles, is a bottle of wine, pinot noir, your favourite varietal, Jacqueline. Go, go and sit down, talk, get to know each other."

***

"I must say," said Jacob, pouring wine into both their glasses, "that you've certainly got a lot of interesting body art."

"These?" Jacqueline shifted a little self-consciously. "Oh, I don't really like them now—a foolish mistake when young and naive."

"I see. Well, I like them. They suit your character, your look." Very boldly, he reached across the table, gently turned one of her wrists over, and examined her tattoos. "Does this give a whole new meaning to trying to read someone?"

He meant it as a joke, but Jacqueline's face creased, showing her displeasure.

"Not really. These are images not words. And I doubt you could make much sense of them." She pointed to the tattoo on her wrist, the head of a dishevelled yet decidedly ordinary looking white man. "Do you know who this is?"

Jacob studied the tattoo again but didn't know who he was supposed to be looking at.

"Erm, he looks familiar but…"

"That's okay. It's not a test," she said in far lighter tones, as if amused by his struggle to identify the man tattooed on her wrist. "This is Lee Harvey Oswald."

"Lee Harvey Oswald? The man who assassinated the President, John F. Kennedy, you mean?"

"That's right."

"But why would you have a tattoo of him on your arm?"

Jacqueline hunched her shoulders. "To be honest, every tattoo I have symbolises something, has a hidden meaning. To be honest, every tattoo I have represents a time when a man has broken my heart."

Jacob didn't know how to take that. Jacqueline had dozens of tattoos on display. And for a man who had never really, truly been in love before, that felt incredibly intimidating. Moreover, he struggled to understand what connection Lee Harvey Oswald could have to any affair of the heart.

"You see," said Jacqueline, "when Oswald assassinated J.F.K., something more than just one man died; the whole world changed, it started a chain of events which culminated in the Vietnam War, one of the cruellest, most senseless of all conflicts, in millions of people losing their lives."

Jacob wasn't sure if he could agree with that.

"Do you really think one man could've stopped a war, though, even the President of the United States?"

"He could've done in my heart, and in my love for him."

"I'm sorry. I don't understand."

"That's what the tattoo symbolises. When my lover left me—and he was my first love—he killed something good and worthy inside, like a pure ideal, a vision of true love, intimacy, something I would never get back. It started a chain of events, a war within myself, and I was never quite the same again."

"Oh, I see," said Jacob. "So his rejection of you was like an assassin's bullet? That's interesting. And who are those two, just below Lee Harvey Oswald?" He touched her arm again, near a tattoo of two women's faces, entwined, fading in and out of each other.

"The first is Zelda Fitzgerald, the second Edie Sedgwick. You've heard of them?"

Jacob wasn't sure if he had but hated the idea of appearing in any way ignorant or behind the times.

"I'm not sure."

"Well, Zelda was the wife of the famous novelist F. Scott Fitzgerald, author of *The Great Gatsby*."

"Ah, of course," said Jacob, "*The Great Gatsby*, the jazz

age, a fabulous book."

"Yes. Yes it is. And I don't know if you were aware, but Zelda had a lot of mental health problems, she ended up in an asylum. By all accounts, she went completely mad—something her husband wrote about in *Tender is the Night*, my favourite book of his. Have you read it?"

"No. No I haven't, unfortunately. My, erm…artistic work has become so time-consuming of late I've neglected my reading terribly."

"Artistic work?"

"Yes. But I don't really like talking about it all that much." Keen to change the subject, he asked, "And why did you choose to get Fitzgerald's wife tattooed onto your arm?"

"Well, after the painful split with my first love, I got involved with another man far too quickly. I was on the rebound I suppose you'd say, vulnerable, and some men have a built-in radar for those they can easily dominate. He was a very handsome man, a brutal, demanding lover, a heavy drug user who got me into some terrible habits. We had a very destructive relationship, one that sent me to the brink of insanity—or so it felt at the time. There was something calculated, almost pathological in the way he treated me, things he would do and say to undermine my confidence, until I became a shambling wreck, completely under his power, until I was no longer master of my own mind. And when I read *Tender is the Night*, and later Zelda's diaries, I really empathised with her struggle with insanity, her struggle to hold onto herself, because it mirrored my own struggle at the time, trying to get that awful man out of my life."

Moved by her words, Jacob reached across the table and touched Jacqueline's hand. In response, she smiled sadly and interlinked her fingers with his, clasping them very tightly.

"And what about the other face, the one next to Zelda's?" He nodded to the second tattoo, that of Edie Sedgwick. "I didn't recognise her name."

"No?" Jacqueline let go of his hand. "Edie was a model and actress who hung around with the artist Andy Warhol, the Factory crowd, in New York in the late sixties, early seventies. I think she had a serious drug problem, but that isn't the reason I had her face tattooed next to Zelda's. No. I identified with Edie because she had an affair with Bob Dylan. I think he really broke her heart. I think he wrote Just Like a Woman about her."

"I know the song," said Jacob, singing: "'She takes just like a woman, she makes love just like a woman, she aches just like a woman, but she breaks just like a little girl.'"

Jacqueline clapped her hands. "You've got a very nice voice, Jacob. And if you like Bob Dylan, that can only be a good thing, another tick in the box."

"The box?"

"Yes. Of things I like about you."

Jacob struggled to keep his composure. Rarely, if ever, had he been in the company of a woman as attractive as Jacqueline. For her to express an interest in him romantically was almost more than he could take.

"So, erm…why did you have the Edie tattoo?"

"Because I've always wanted to fall in love with someone talented, an artist, someone famous and revered. I've always wanted to be a muse, to inspire such passion in a great man that he'd want to write about me, paint me, sculpt me, sing about me, but, unfortunately, I…I never have."

Jacob felt sad to hear Jacqueline talk like that, but hopeful for himself nonetheless, thinking that perhaps he might be the kind of artist she could truly fall in love with.

"And this one," said Jacqueline, pointing to the next tattoo, an elegant dancing woman enveloped in a cloud of miasmic smoke, "this is of Salome."

"Salome?"

"The step-daughter of King Herod, the man who ordered Jesus' crucifixion. By all accounts, she was a great beauty and wonderful dancer, whom Herod was infatuated with. One night, and please forgive me, I may have the events a little muddled, Herod granted her a wish, and she asked for the head of John the Baptist."

Having never taken that much interest in religious matters, he again felt a little lost and out of his depth.

"And what does her tattoo symbolise?"

"Oh, it's quite simple. In my foolishness, I allowed that horrible, manipulative man"—she tapped Zelda Fitzgerald's face—"back into my life. What a fool I was! What a nightmare I endured—for almost eighteen months. And one morning, in the early hours, after he'd brutalised me on every possible level—mentally, physically, sexually—I got out of bed, went downstairs, and sat in the dark, cold, quiet of my front room. From out of the shadows appeared a beautiful dancing shape, a vision of Salome, I was certain of it. And she, just like Herod, granted me one wish, and with all my heart, I wanted that bastard who was snoring away upstairs head on a platter." She stared into space for a moment. "A few hours later, I bagged up all his belongings, told him to leave and never come back. Incredibly, he put up little resistance, which I attributed to Salome's mystical influence. To mark what I considered to be a hugely courageous move on my behalf, I cleared out my savings account, went to the tattoo parlour, and had her tattooed on my arm. Now I see it as a symbol of my inner strength, the person I know I can be if I truly put my mind to it."

They fell silent for a few moments, each having a sip of wine.

"I hope I haven't come across as especially bitter, Jacob. It's just that I've had so many bad experiences with men. But I hate being on my own. I hate being single. And I think you and I would make a good couple. We have lots in common. I love art, music, going to gigs, festivals. Maybe, later in the summer, we could go somewhere together, even if it was just to a club that played our kinds of songs."

"Yes, I'd really like that," said Jacob, almost overwhelmed by the prospect. This evening, he had only come out for a quiet drink; now he was in the throes of embarking upon a relationship with a beautiful, alluring young woman. "Although, I must admit, I'm not in the best position financially, earnings from my artistic work can be very sporadic, but I feel close to some kind of breakthrough, so it won't be like this forever."

"I understand," she said. "Money isn't everything."

Padded footfalls sounded against the stone flooring. Both turned to see Hans walking over on his hind legs.

"Sorry to interrupt, Jacqueline," he said. "But we must leave soon." He touched her shoulder. "Have you enjoyed yourself?"

"Very much," she said, smiling. "I'm so glad you telephoned."

Hans turned and winked at Jacob.

"That's great," he said. "Call it a sixth sense, but I had a feeling you two would hit it off. Therefore, only one question remains: does Jacob Fallada warrant a second date? Does Jacqueline want to see him again?"

Jacob felt momentarily panicked. He had really enjoyed talking to Jacqueline tonight, and had no idea that she planned to leave so early, or that the question of them seeing each other again (which he was keen to do) would be brought up in such a clinical manner.

"Well, that depends entirely upon Jacob," she said, very seriously. "If he's willing to make the obligatory concessions then I would be more than happy to see him on a regular basis."

"'Obligatory concessions'?" he said, confused.

"That's right," Hans spoke for her. "Jacqueline insists that all her prospective partners have a tattoo of her face scraped across their skin. Not right away, of course." He smiled blankly and hunched his shoulders. "But as long as an oral agreement is reached at this juncture, you will be able to see Jacqueline again. So, Jacob, are you willing to comply?"

"Yes, yes I am," he blurted out, even though the thought of a tattooist's needle filled him with dread. "I…I can't see that being a problem."

"Excellent." Jacqueline got to her feet. "If you're not busy tomorrow morning, we can meet at the pig circus in town. I hear a young swine is being tried in the churchyard, an intriguing case. There are always lots of people around, and maybe afterwards, we could have a drink and a bite to eat."

"The pig circus?" Jacob tried to mask his distaste. This barbaric tradition, blaming an innocent pig for a natural disaster, dressing it up in human clothes, and then hanging it, was, to his mind, completely wrong. "Erm, okay. Maybe we can go along and watch for a while. And like you say, we can always call in somewhere for a drink and a bite to eat later."

"That's settled, then," said Hans. "Tomorrow morning, you will meet up with Jacqueline for your first official date."

***

Arriving a little late, Jacob missed the main proceedings, which had been conducted inside the church itself.

By word of mouth, listening to those gathered, he learned that a large white breed pig had been found guilty of coastal erosion, of causing part of the cliff tops just outside town to collapse into the sea.

"That ruddy porker," said one crotchety old man, "he were responsible for that east cliff falling onto the beach, don't you worry 'bout that."

Almost by chance, Jacob bumped into Jacqueline as she stood scanning the crowds, as if looking for someone in particular.

"Oh, hello, Jacob, right on time," she said, looking past him, over his shoulder. "Thank you for coming."

"Thank you for inviting me. Are…Are you all right? You seem a little distracted."

"What?" Giving a start, she turned and stared right into his eyes, put both hands on his face, and kissed him passionately. This went on for several minutes. When she finally disengaged, she immediately scanned the crowds again.

Jacob grabbed her elbow. "Jacqueline, what was that all—?" a blast from a trumpet cut him short.

Both turned to see a pig being roughly escorted from the church. Two huge, lumbering, masked executioners, barearmed, dressed in leather aprons, had a vise-like grip of the animal. Squealing, walking on its hind legs, attired in a shiny black tuxedo, the pig struggled to shake itself free. As the men dragged it closer towards the gallows, the townsfolk, faces creased in anger, shouted vociferous obscenities and pelted the animal with rotten fruit and vegetables.

"You bastard!"

"Cliff killer!"

"Scourge of the coast!"

"Hang the swine!"

Side on, one of the executioners put a foot on the first

step leading up to the gallows. Inexplicably (for these men were famed for their professionalism), he stumbled slightly, loosening his grip on the pig. In turn, his colleague, not expecting any mishap, stumbled too, falling down to one knee. Taking full advantage, the pig shook itself free and made a dash across the churchyard, bundling its way through the aggressive, baying crowd, knocking young and old to the ground, bloodying knees and elbows.

"You slippery swine!"

"You perfidious porker!"

"You hateful hog!"

Doomed to failure, such were the numbers of people blocking any clear path to escape, the pig was eventually tripped and halted directly in front of Jacob and Jacqueline. Writhing, pinned to the ground by many vengeful hands, the animal looked right into Jacob's eyes, and pleaded with him to intercede.

"You must help me!" it gasped. "You know I can't be guilty of such an absurd crime. You know that coastal erosion is due to irrigation, water off the land, as much as the sea itself. It is, to all intents and purposes, an act of God."

There was such terror in the pig's eyes, Jacob had to look away.

"Lift him up," shouted one of the townsfolk, encouraging a large group to grab the pig and hoist it aloft their shoulders. "Let's get him up to those gallows. Let's hang the bastard by the neck."

Jacob kept his eyes lowered as they marched the pig all the way up to the gallows, handing him to the two crestfallen executioners (such blunders were not tolerated; both men knew, therefore, that this was very likely to be their last ever execution). With a roughness proportionate to their disappointment, they stood the pig on a wooden stool, and put a thick length of hempen rope around its neck.

"Now," one of the executioners said into a loudspeaker. "This porker has been found guilty of willfully destroying our beautiful cliff tops. Therefore, it must be hung from the neck until it is dead."

The crowd roared its approval. Grown men and women, pensioners, spotty teens, children, some no more than five or six years of age, raised their fists, spat and cursed, wolf-whistled or blew into elaborate home-made vuvuzelas. Horrified, Jacob buried his face in his hands, just as the stool was knocked out from under the pig, just as he heard the snap of the noose, and an awful breathless squealing as the animal's neck was no doubt broken.

When he lifted his head, Jacqueline was nowhere to be seen.

***

As the crowds dispersed, he saw her talking to a skinny, dark-haired young man, attired in the standard tracksuit bottoms and string vest, and who had many colourful tattoos running up and down his arms.

"Jacqueline?" Jacob shouted out.

She swung round, and when seeing him, quickly whispered something to the young man, who nodded and shuffled away, joining the many departing bodies. To Jacob's shock, he saw that the tattoos running up and down his arms were similar to Jacqueline's, that they were all of faces, some of whom he recognised: Medusa, Charles Manson, Margaret Thatcher, and most strikingly of all, one of Jacqueline herself.

"I lost you in the crowd," he said. "I didn't know where you'd got to. And I can't say I particularly enjoyed the hanging. I don't think that kind of thing has any place in modern society."

Jacqueline clicked her tongue and put her hands on her hips. "Is that all you can talk about—the pig circus?"

"I…I don't understand."

"No, clearly you don't," she said, scowling. "Last night, I outlined the basic requirements on which our relationship would be founded. But I have serious doubts as to whether you have made the necessary arrangements yet."

"What? A tattoo, you mean?"

"Of course. I can't waste time like this, Jacob. Each moment is precious. If you're not serious about me then I'm afraid our relationship will have to end before it's even begun."

"What? But I thought we were going out with each other now. I thought you really liked me. I thought you said we made a really good couple."

Jacqueline didn't respond; she just stood there, tapping her foot, as if she really wanted to be somewhere else.

It was then a horrible sense of realisation fell in on Jacob. The tattooed young man from a moment ago, who was he? Jacqueline's former lover?

"Wait. Who was that man, the one you were talking to?"

Jacqueline's face betrayed something guilty and ashamed. Very slowly, she rolled up her sleeve and pointed to the Lee Harvey Oswald tattoo.

"As I told you, this is a symbol of the only man I'll ever love."

"What?"

"Go home, Jacob. You can be of no further use to me."

8

The Music of Chance

Jacob Fallada recognised Michela Murphy as soon as she walked into the busy coffee shop. Since their school days, she hadn't changed all that much. She was still an attractive, stylish young woman, only now, in the prime of her life, walking arm-in-arm with an equally stylish, disarmingly handsome man. In the past, Jacob had always been fascinated by the nimbus-like glow that shone from the beautiful and successful amongst us. Such preordained favour made him seriously question whether his whole existence hadn't been a spiteful charade, a mocking repudiation of things he knew he would never have, as if he had only pursued an artistic life as a kind of excuse, a disclaimer, and would've traded every single piece of artwork he'd ever created if he could live just one day in the shoes of Michela Murphy's lover.

As quickly as they had appeared, the golden couple disappeared amongst the crowds queuing in front of a team of highly skilled but incredibly temperamental baristas.

And Jacob thought that was that. That he had got a brief

glimpse into the not completely unexpectedly wonderful life of the always popular and attractive Michela Murphy, and that he wouldn't see her again for another decade or two, but that didn't prove to be the case.

"Jacob, Jacob Fallada." Michela had quickly returned, perhaps in search of an empty table.

He tried to look surprised, to perhaps even feign ignorance, as if he wasn't quite sure who this beautiful young woman was.

"It's me, Michela, Michela Murphy from school."

"Oh yes, of course." He nodded and half-smiled in pretence of welcome recognition. "I was miles away. You know how it is."

"You always were the big dreamer, Jacob, with a mind full of artistic ideas, weren't you?" On the half-turn, she ushered her partner over. "Richard, I'd like you to meet an old school friend of mine, Jacob Fallada."

"Nice to meet you, Jacob. I would shake your hand but…" he gave the tray he was holding a little levitation as if to exonerate himself from any formal handshaking duties.

"Nice to meet you, Richard," he said, presuming they would swoon off now and find somewhere to sit on their own. But, incredibly, Michela insisted that she and her fiancé join Jacob at his table for a chat.

"Would be so nice to catch up, wouldn't it?" she said, with the kind of enthusiasm that was either insincere or completely misplaced.

"Erm, yes," said Jacob, "yes, it would."

Not that he felt completely comfortable with the situation. Throughout the early part of the conversation, dominated by Michela, he could never quite tell if they were making fun of him or not. On occasion he thought that he caught them exchanging a patronising grin or a facetious rolling of the eyes. But there was something indefatigable about Michela's pleasant chit-chit, the constant references to their school days, fearsome old teachers, that told Jacob that this couldn't be the case, simply because she was going to far too much trouble for a bit of simple teasing, putting far too much of herself out there. Mockery should, after all, be a leisurely pursuit.

"Oh, and do you remember that time those horrible boys at school threw me in that ditch?"

Jacob nearly choked on his coffee. That particular incident was the last thing he thought Michela would bring up in front of the man she clearly wanted to spend the rest of her life with.

"It's such a funny story, Richard. Can't believe I haven't told you before." She shook her head and smiled ruefully. "You know what my parents are like, even now—pseudo-intellectual progressives, reading all these books on radical thought. Well, when me and Jacob were about thirteen, fourteen years old…"

And she went on to tell Richard the whole story, how those older boys had thrown her into the ditch, how she suffered quite serious spinal injuries, injuries that could very well have confined her to a wheelchair for life, how she put the blame solely onto Jacob because she didn't want such rough ignorant characters in her house, participating in her father's stupid 'social reprogramming scheme', how he made Jacob act like a dog for three whole weeks, ferrying her meals up and down the stairs, relieving himself outside, sleeping in what amounted to a booby-trapped basket and having to suffer water aversion therapy and the occasional jab from an electric taser.

"Wow." Richard rocked back in his chair. "That's absolute madness."

"It was." She chuckled and squeezed his hand. "They're such fruitcakes, my folks. I felt so awful about everything, Jacob. And I'm sorry if I was a bitch to you. But I'd been cooped up in hospitals, wearing full body casts and back braces for weeks. I was at the end of my tether, I really was."

"No, no, I understand," he lied, all the bitterness he had repressed for years having been stirred up by her story. "It was a little extreme at the time, but no harm done."

"And didn't you wind them up in the end," she asked, "by pretending to act like a dog, long after the three weeks were up? Classic."

No, he would dearly have loved to have contradicted her, *I was severely traumatised by the whole experience. It took six weeks before I could speak again, and another fortnight before I was able to walk on two feet, like a normal, functioning human being.*

Michela changed the subject.

"You used to live with your aunt, didn't you? How is she these days?"

"Dead, I'm afraid," he said with a certain relish, sure it would wipe the complacent look from her face. But no. She took it in her ultra-confident, diplomatic stride.

"I'm so sorry to hear that. I can't remember her too well, but I'm sure she was a lovely woman."

There was a momentary lull in conversation. A cash register clattered open. A baby's cry was quickly subdued. The coffee machines spluttered and frothed.

"And what do you do with yourself these days, Jacob?" asked Michela. "You have a very, erm...bohemian look about you, so I'm guessing you're still ploughing the artistic furrow, as it were."

"Yes, that's right, still plugging away, still getting up each morning, still working on what has become a pretty long-term project now."

"Oh, that's interesting," said Richard, for the first time actively participating in the conversation. "What sort of stuff do you do?"

"Well." Jacob screwed up his face. He reached for his cup only to put it straight back down again. "It's not easy to define, categorise, or put into any kind of box," he said, paraphrasing Rhea Hilton from another lifetime ago. "I tend to splice genres, mix things up—part painter, part writer, part candlestick maker."

There was a brief, slightly uncomfortable pause before both Richard and Michela snorted with laughter.

"Hey, nice play on words," said Richard, patting Jacob's shoulder. "Must be great, though, living in a nice, peaceful area like this, being a local artist, taking your inspiration from such picturesque surroundings."

"Actually, Richard is from around this neck of the woods too, aren't you, darling?" Michela didn't wait for him to confirm as much. "Only he's a few years older than us and educated out at Greshams, the clever clogs. But you used to spend all your summers with your grandmother in town, didn't you?"

"Indeed I did," said Richard. "Haven't been back for years, though, what with my P.H.D., working overseas, and my short stint at the Home Office. And I know the town has gone to rack and ruin, that it looks a bit tatty in places now, economic downturn and all that, but I've still got a lot of affection for the place. Lots of good memories are tied up here. Especially the summers down on the beach. Me and my friends had the best times. Only…Ha!" he trailed off into reflective, head-shaking laughter.

"What is it?" Michela prompted, as if the relay of one of her memories deserved one of his in return.

"Only a very unpleasant thing happened to me one summer." He raised a hand towards his forehead only to quickly lower it again. "Funny how certain incidents just pop back into you mind, isn't it? But when we took a stroll along the promenade earlier, it all came flooding back to me."

"What came flooding back to you?" Michela persisted.

"Haven't I told you this before? About that time when I was about twelve, thirteen and that little boy threw a massive rock at me, splitting my head open."

Jacob felt a cold, ugly feeling come over him, like the onset of a fever, like figurative germs were multiplying in the deepest, darkest recesses of his mind. Surely Richard wasn't the boy he had thrown a rock at all those years ago. It was too random and coincidental, to be reunited like this, after such a long time.

"Really?" asked Michela.

"Yeah, here, look." He pulled up his floppy fringe and showed her a small yet discernible scar. "My mum told me it was just a scratch, but I actually needed a few stitches to seal the cut and suffered from terrible headaches for the rest of the holidays."

"What, erm…actually happened?" asked Jacob.

"Well, it must've been mid-August time…"

And Richard set the scene, describing the glorious sunshine, the sound of the surf, shrill laughter, excited voices, he named all of his friends present, how they'd devised this ingenious way of filling a rock pool when the tide was coming in, diverting the water with irrigation channels made out of boulders gathered from the beach, so they had their own giant paddling pool, and how this little boy kept pestering them.

"He was a hell of a state, frail, skinny, emaciated, you

could see his ribs protruding through the skin, could only have been four or five years old, a bit dirty, scummy, you know, long greasy hair, and he was running around in a pair of tatty old underpants instead of trunks. We all felt sorry for him. He looked so isolated and alone. And he badly wanted to join in with what we were doing, but we wouldn't let him. And I think he got really upset about it." He sighed and shook his head. "But what he didn't understand was that the water was too deep. First and foremost, we didn't want him to get hurt, to drown, even. We were only so off-hand with him for his own safety. But he persisted, he kept on and on, poor little guy, and with us being older, full of bravado, I suppose we were a bit cruel to him, telling him to go away and play on his own."

All the time Richard narrated his version of events, Jacob felt as if he was back on the beach that day, seeing things from the older boy's point of view, as if he was trawling over Jacob's most affecting memories in the same way a fishing net trawls the seabed, disturbing everything in its wake, stirring up clouds of sand with a snow-globe effect. Only Jacob wasn't sure how his memory of that day would appear when everything had settled, when Richard's story was over.

"Anyway," he resumed after a sip of coffee, "we didn't think any more of it, we continued to run around, to dive in the rock pool, having the time of our lives. But that little boy, he must've brooded on things. Because he picked up a sizeable stone, calmly walked over to us and threw it right into the heart of the group, hitting me clean on the side of the head."

"That sounds a bit extreme," said Jacob, unable to stop himself, "—throwing a stone at you just because you told him he couldn't play with you. Are you sure you didn't do anything else to antagonise him? Physically assault him, perhaps? Maybe even interfere with his own attempts at installing a drainage channel?"

Richard looked at Jacob askance.

"No, no…not that I recall. He just ran up to us and threw the rock, knocking me down onto my backside. Can't tell you how shocked I was. One minute, laughing and messing around with my pals. The next, rolling around on the sand, crying my eyes out, with this massive cut spurting blood all over the place."

"Oh, that must've been terrible," said Michela, "—the shock, I mean."

"It was—can still remember it so vividly," he replied. "The pain that wouldn't seem to go away, the choking tears, the way my heart was pounding against my chest. But more than anything, I've always wondered what he must've been thinking, that little boy, what had been going through his head. Not why he picked up the stone and threw it in the first place—we knew why he did that—but afterwards, when he realised what he'd done. I always wondered whether he felt bad about it or not, guilty, ashamed, whether he knew that he'd just done something so, so wrong."

Michela squeezed his hand again, as if he had just said something very profound.

"It's interesting, isn't it? I read somewhere that there are lobes at the front of the brain, controlling our ability to make judgements between what is right and wrong that don't develop until we're fourteen or fifteen. That's why children should never, ever be tried as adults in court, no matter how terrible a crime they've committed."

Jacob had never heard anything like that before. And in an odd, contrary way, it made him feel a little bit better about his part in the incident, because, if Michela was correct, he wasn't responsible for his actions, after all.

"The funny thing was," said Richard, "that little boy, he just up and disappeared, like literally vanished into thin air. I remember my friends dashing around, looking for him. I remember them telling my mother how this skinny little kid had just run over and thrown a stone at us, that he'd known exactly what he was doing, but, like I said, no one could find him."

"And what do you think would've happened if he hadn't have disappeared like that?" asked Jacob, desperate to find out, to fill a missing space in his memory. Because although, for him, the incident had no immediate consequences, in terms of punishment, on a far greater, deeper level, he had suffered for it way beyond a mere telling-off or slap on the wrists. "Would you have, erm…I don't know, taken him to the police station, maybe even pressed—?"

"Oh, God no," said Richard. "I think, after the shock had worn off, I'd have wanted to have sat him down and spoken to him, you know, given him like a big brother chat, asking him why he did what he did, and, of course, telling him that he shouldn't throw stones at people, that it was dangerous, that someone could've gotten seriously hurt."

"You'd have wanted to befriend him?" asked Jacob.

Richard took a moment to ponder this.

"You know, I think I probably would, strange as it sounds. I've learnt in life that all people need is a kind word, someone to reach out and offer them a little human kindness, and it can turn their entire lives around."

Long after Michela and Richard had taken their leave, Jacob remained in the coffee shop, replaying Richard's version of events through his head. Things which had festered with him for decades, black, ugly thoughts rotting in the depths of his mind had had new, clean, reinvigorating life breathed into them. Now Jacob viewed that day completely different-ly. Clearly, painfully almost, he saw himself remaining there on the beach, walking over to the injured boy, apologising profusely to him, his mother and friends. He saw them all turn around and look at him, but not in anger or recrimina-tion, but with compassion and understanding. He saw him and Richard (head swathed in bandages) sitting on a bank of shingle and stone, having the 'big brother' chat that Rich-ard had mentioned, the older boy putting his arm around Jacob's thin shoulders, imparting sage advice, taking him under his wing, offering to become his friend and men-tor. More fancifully, he saw himself walking around town with Richard, visiting the amusement arcades, eating fish and chips, even sitting around a table enjoying a meal with his family, laughing and joking about the stone-throwing incident that had brought them all together. And finally, as if Jacob as seven-year-old boy had come full circle, he saw himself on the beach with his older friends, gathering boul-ders and constructing a drainage channel.

Is that what life is all about, Jacob thought to himself, a series of stolen, misplaced opportunities, where we are but one moment away from true, lasting happiness, a moment away from forging unshakeable human bonds, a moment away from love, romance, intimacy? If so, was the process perpetual, constant? Were there things to be optimistic about? Could life yet deliver to Jacob Fallada all that he had been looking for ever since he was a little boy?

Maybe if he hadn't been so affected by the chance meeting with Michela and Richard, maybe if Richard's story hadn't had such a profound, diverting impact, Ja-cob wouldn't have aimlessly wandered into such a danger-ous situation, he wouldn't have attempted to cut through the back of the supermarket car park, a notorious area at night, invariably populated by hooded youths smoking and drinking themselves senseless. In many ways, therefore, Jacob had to take some responsibility for what happened to him. If only he had his wits about him, none of what followed need to have happened.

Another, far less edifying, twist of fate.

***

"Oi, geezer," came a mockney-accented voice from the shadows. "Scruff-bag, Mr Scarecrow Man."

Jacob gave a start, stopped and turned around. If he squinted up his eyes in the darkness, he could just about make out a few human shapes loitering beside a giant builder's skip.

"Yeah, that's right. You. Come over here. I need a favour. It's an emergency, life or bloody death."

Almost involuntarily, in direct contravention of all concepts of self-preservation and common sense, Jacob found himself walking into the shadowy depths, closer to the skip.

"Yes," he said, peering into those ambiguous shades of the night.

There were seven, maybe eight young people standing under a huge cloud of smoke, Hiroshima in miniature.

"We're hungry," said who was clearly the ringleader, a boy of indeterminate years—he could've been eleven, he could've been eighteen—dressed in baggy clothing and a baseball cap. "Give us a tenner for a kebab, will you, chief?"

"No, no, I'm sorry," said Jacob, backing away. "You've got the wrong man. I have very little by way of money on me. I'm a local artist. I—"

"Shut your neck!"

From all sides, at a rapid and stealthy rate, like a team of crack marksmen attending a hostage situation, the gang surrounded Jacob. It was then he felt fear, real, genuine fear, because he knew that through his own stupid self-absorbed naivety, he had just stumbled into a very dangerous situation, one it might not be easy to extricate himself from. But it was more than just fear that pulsed through him in those early moments of dire realisation, it was disgust, disappointment, because these feral street urchins represented everything he hated most about life: ignorance, crassness, violence, inarticulateness, ugly normality, the devolution of the species.

"An artist, are you?"

The boy lunged forward, grabbing Jacob by the collar and roughly pushing him up against the supermarket's red-bricked wall.

"What kind of artist?"

"I...I sketch, draw," Jacob grimaced and groaned, his face pressed tightly against cold, rough, flaky stone, "but... but I don't like to talk about my work all that much."

"Oh, you don't, do you? No worry. Like we give a fuck about your art. Art's for cunts. All we're concerned about is sorting out these munchies. Now, where's your money? Where's your wallet, Mr Artist Man?"

"I told you. I haven't got very much money, almost nothing, in fact."

"Don't give me that bollocks!" he said, spraying Jacob's cheek with a pinprick burst of warm spittle spray. "You artists and writers are bloody loaded, millionaires most of you, sitting in your luxury houses, sipping champagne. Now, where's your fucking dough?"

"Really, no, I'm telling the truth, I—"

"Greeny," the boy said over his shoulder. "Shake this muppet down, will you?"

Another boy appeared at Jacob's side in an almost spectral puff of what was undoubtedly cannabis smoke. With no hesitation, with the rapid, proficient thoroughness of a seasoned security guard, he started to pat Jacob's pockets, to drag his bag from his shoulder, to rifle through his note- and sketchbooks, to empty the contents out on to the pavement.

"Forty-eight pence."

"You what?" cried the ringleader.

"Yeah, that's all he's got on him, man—forty-eight-fuck-ing-pence."

"You're taking the piss, Mr Artist Man." Gripping Jacob's collar, the youth brought his neck back and butted Jacob in the nose with his forehead, sending a spray of blood, membrane and bone spattering high into the air.

After that, Jacob could remember little of the vicious attack. In all likelihood (well, that was how it was explained to him in the hospital during the early days of his recovery), he slipped in and out of consciousness many times. Only one sickeningly vivid detail stayed with him throughout his ordeal, throughout every kick and punch: the dog. Although he hadn't noticed it before, one of the gang had a squat, muscular fighting dog on a leash. And the more brutal and prolonged the attack, the more agitated this animal became. At one time, it was so close to Jacob he could feel the warmth of its breath, could see thick arrows of drool dangling from its fearsome jaws. It kept rearing up, straining at the leash, barking, growling, seething with a contained devastation desperate for outlet. If it could've got at him it would've torn him to pieces, it would've ripped his face clean off. And perversely, terrifyingly, the youths (children, they were no more than children) were incredibly amused by this. So much so, they kept prodding and poking the snapping, snarling hound, working it up into a frenzy, as if they really did mean to let it off the leash at any second. And that's the one thing that kept going through Jacob's head, Please, not the dog, anything but the dog…

And then, from out of this wild maelstrom of horrible confusion, a bastardised cacophony of savage sound and demented movement, everything slowed…And then everything went dark…And then Jacob saw himself on the beach as a little boy again, watching that stone arc and dip through the air in slow motion…

9

Gradual Epiphany

Jacob Fallada was woken by a light knocking on the caravan door. Dearly, he wished he hadn't engaged the lock overnight; then he wouldn't have had to haul himself up off the tatty, torn banquette that served as his sick bed. Ever since the attack, Jacob had been incredibly unsteady on his feet, doddery almost, forgetful, distant to himself, like an old man with the onset of dementia. It was far more than just physical, though. Never the most sociable or confident of characters, he was too scared to venture into town now. He jumped at every sound. He suffered from excruciatingly vivid nightmares, flashbacks of the attack itself. Most worryingly of all, he found it increasingly difficult to work. His hands shook so violently, he could barely hold a pencil, pen, or paintbrush for more than a few minutes at a time. And it was this, more than anything else, that had drained Jacob Fallada of all spirit, all enthusiasm for life.

Eventually, using the dining-table for support, he managed to turn the flimsy plastic lock, opening the door.

"Oh, hello, Mr Fallada," said local care worker Yvonne Nicholson, with what Jacob took as forced breeziness. "I hope I haven't interrupted anything. But we are scheduled for another meeting this morning."

All his life, Jacob had been able to gauge the exact level of a person's dislike towards him by their facial expression. In everyday situations, he had always picked up on certain momentary lapses, a lowering of the eyes or wrinkling of the nose, which told him exactly how that person was thinking or feeling at any given time. This morning, the grave, pitying, almost tearful look on Yvonne Nicholson's face told him that his condition had visibly worsened. Then again, he knew the place was filthy, he knew there were cups and dishes piled up in the sink and dirty clothes strewn across the floor, he knew there was little or no ventilation here, that the air was almost fetid, that his living conditions were truly pitiful.

"Please, come in," he said, backing away from the door, and sliding into a seat at the dining-table. "Sorry I was a little slow answering. I've not been feeling too sharp these last few days, not been able to get about much."

"Are you having the dizzy spells again?" She slipped her bag off her shoulder and sat opposite him. "If you ever get like that, you should try and lie down. We don't want you having another fall now, do we?"

"No, of course not." He smiled blankly. "And have you heard anything back regarding my claim?"

"Things aren't looking too good, I'm afraid. As you haven't ever paid any tax or national insurance, you aren't entitled to free healthcare. Therefore, you're going to have to pay for the medication you require. Which, we both know, you're not in a position to do. I really feel for you, Jacob. I mean, you were the victim of a brutal attack by a vicious gang of drug- and drink-addled youths, left almost for dead. And when you're finally rushed to hospital for emergency surgery, you contract Hep C through a botched blood transfusion. How unlucky can a person get?"

Jacob couldn't help but laugh. Not that the precarious state of his health amused him; he just didn't know what else to do anymore.

"But we're not without hope." Yvonne took some papers out of her bag. "I made a few enquiries and you may be eligible for a small support stipend, paid direct into the post office each month. So, if I could just get you to read these forms." She laid a thick wad of papers out on the table. "And then sign them. I can pop them in the post this afternoon."

"Okay. Great. I'll do that now."

While Jacob read through the relevant documentation, Yvonne gave the caravan a thorough clean, doing all the washing-up, placing each cup, plate and piece of cutlery in the relevant cupboard or drawer, picking up all his dirty clothes and folding them up on the banquette, airing his bedding, sweeping the floor and opening the door a crack, to provide some much-needed ventilation.

By the time she had finished, Jacob was putting his signature to the application form.

"What's this here?" she asked, picking up a beautiful charcoal sketch of a dilapidated caravan in a secluded clearing with the words Gradual Epiphany printed at the bottom. "Is this one of your own pictures, Jacob? Are all these yours?" She pointed to the pile stacked on the table.

"Yes, yes they are," he said, putting pen and papers aside. "In the corner"—he turned and pointed—"over there, and behind the curtain, are what constitutes my life's work. Not that anybody has ever, or will ever, see it in now. Seems like such a waste."

"Well, I'm somebody, aren't I? Why don't you show me a few of your other pictures, like my own personal exhibition? I'd love to see what you've been up to all these years."

Even though Jacob sensed that Yvonne was only showing an interest to be kind, even though he knew she wasn't the right person to critique his work, he now realised (or had come to appreciate, especially in the weeks and months after the attack), that if you wait for the perfect moment in life, there's a good chance that it might never come around.

"Okay," he said. "I'd like that." He sorted through the pile of sketches on the desk. "But firstly, to give you an idea of how I work, I better explain something. You see this picture here?"

He held up a child's drawing, full of bright bold colours—yellows, oranges, blues—a beach scene, complete with sea, sand and sun. At the bottom of the picture, in squiggly yet legible words: The Day I Threw the Rock.

"This is the first picture I ever drew, aged seven," he explained, "on the day I realised that I wanted to become an artist. Fast-forward ten years, and you have this."

He held up another picture, in charcoal, exquisite in its fine detail and subtle smudging, a picture of a teenage boy, writhing around on the sand, with what looked like a nasty cut to his forehead.

Yvonne took the picture and studied it at closer quarters.

"That's amazing, Jacob. It looks so...so real, so harrowing and alive. And what's that at the bottom?—some verse."

The first thud of awakening,
A realisation of what we are all truly capable of,
A showdown with self, the latent darkness
That festers in the distant recesses of even the most timorous heart.

"By age fourteen," Jacob moved on, not wanting to linger on words he had written so many years ago, "I had come a long way, had developed both as a person and fledgling artist. This picture predates the one I just showed you, but is, in many ways, more representative of the period in which I discovered my own true style, the kind of emotional territory I wanted to concentrate on."

He handed Yvonne another charcoal sketch of the same high quality, the same delicate beauty, a picture of a skinny young boy struggling across a muddy sports field. In this picture, Jacob had cleverly positioned this tiny figure against a towering backdrop—the cloudy grey sky, the sweeping rain, the surrounding woodland—creating a strong, bleak, compelling impression of isolation, helplessness even, the sense that this boy wasn't just trekking across a muddy sports field at the height of winter, but through life itself, with all its painful trials and tribulations.

"And this next one I call Of Christians and Cannibals."

"Of Christians and Cannibals?" She laughed. "That's a rather unusual title, and rather unusual bedfellows."

"Are they? Really? I'm not so sure. In my life, the very worst people I've encountered are those who have masqueraded as respectable and virtuous, when really, behind closed doors, at heart, they're the most wretched, deceitful creatures on earth."

Clearly taken aback, Yvonne stared at a startling, almost terrifying close-up image of a woman's face twisted with anger, twisted out of all proportion, her great big eyes bulging in each socket. For additional effect, Jacob had added a pop-art, Roy Lichtenstein-style speech bubble:

Yeah, your kind—scruffy, grubby perverts, sex fiends,

paedophiles

Which only added to the power of the picture, like a piece of scathing social commentary.

"And here," he said, sliding another sketch from the pile, "we have a picture of a very special person. I know it doesn't look very flattering. I know that if a man had sketched you in such a manner you'd probably be hugely offended. But believe me, the woman in question, probably the love of my life—a very much unrequited, unconsummated, one-sided love, I might add—would understand completely. For I adored every inch of her soft warm flesh."

He passed Yvonne a picture of a skinny, misshapen woman in glasses sitting astride a chair, her floppy breasts dangling down, a far from flattering rendition, as Jacob rightly said, but there was a tenderness to the image, a sense of intimacy, an unguarded moment captured, something shared between two people who trusted and understood each other completely.

"I actually wrote lots of verse about her, even though we only knew each other intimately for a short period, maybe a month. Here, there's something on the back, I believe, a short poem."

Hopeful Hopelessness
if you write about something so intently,
so tenderly and passionately,
are you not only keeping it alive
but trying to bring it back to life?

"That's beautiful—lovelorn, full of yearning. You really are quite the wordsmith. I had no idea that you wrote as well as sketched and painted. I never knew you had such a huge body of work, that you'd accomplished so much in your life."

"'Accomplished?'" He hunched his shoulders. "That's what's always fascinated me. When does the art or the artwork, the writer or book, really exist?—the moment it's painted or written, or the moment it comes to the public's attention? By that I mean, should the artist or writer not feel immense satisfaction in the act of creation itself, regardless of success, recognition, cultural sainthood?"

"I don't know, Jacob. But a work of art can't go on to garner universal acclaim if it doesn't exist in the first place, can it? The picture has to be painted, the book has to be written first."

"I agree." He picked up another sketch. "Oh, and here, this is a drawing I made of my aunt. She, erm…hadn't been well, had, in fact, just passed away. But, curiously enough, at the moment of death, her eyes remained wide open. And I don't know what it was, but I saw more life in them then than I ever had during all the years she lived."

In this picture, Jacob had left his aunt's face almost untouched, like a blank canvas, and focused solely on the eyes, capturing a soft, wanton tenderness, a longing for life that had passed forever more. In that respect, it contrasted sharply with the sketch of the woman in the street, deranged with anger, but was a mesmerising picture in its own right, one hard to tear yourself away from, the kind of picture in which you find some new and compelling detail each time you look at it.

"And this next one captures one of the most curious incidents of my life. I call it Three Little Boys."

It was a smudgy yet effective representation of three young boys emerging through a curtain of mist. For reasons not immediately apparent, there was an element of menace about these children, despite the fact they were wearing bobble-hats and scarves and wellington boots to protect them from the elements. Only when Yvonne looked closer did she notice that the boys were holding something in their hands. Knives. No. Protractors.

"Why are they armed like that, Jacob? Are you trying to get across some sense of school bullying?"

He didn't know what to say to that, so, from memory, he recited the poem that was printed at the bottom of the picture.

Through a truant dawn,
Old torments return.
Painful memories will continue to haunt,
Until you are strong enough to let go of the past.

Keen to move on again, Jacob picked up yet another sketch.

"And this one is even more curious."

"How'd you mean?"

"Well, have you ever encountered a talking dog?"

She laughed once more. "No, I can't say I have."

"But the oddest things do happen, from time to time. And you meet such strange and damaged people in this life, don't you?—people like Jacqueline."

"Jacqueline?"

"That's right." He handed Yvonne a sketch of Jacqueline's exquisite face. "She has a tattoo of Lee Harvey Oswald on her wrist, to signify a broken heart."

"A what on her wrist?"

Jacob chuckled, reached across the table, and turned the sketch Yvonne was holding around.

"Is this another of your poems?"

Your book's cover
Is your body's art
A cruel, calculated betrayal
From deep within your damaged heart

Once again, he reached across the table only to hesitate, to take the next sketch and slide it to the bottom of the pile.

"It's perhaps best that I don't show you that one."

"Why?"

"It's something from the night of the attack. I…I'd rather not, that's all. It's still too raw and painful, something I don't feel ready sharing yet."

They lapsed into silence for a moment.

"So, let me get this straight, Jacob, you've actually documented every incident from your life with a picture and an accompanying poem? Are they poems?"

"Well, some might call them haikus, or something of the like. They're short, perhaps insubstantial in many ways, as I feel a lot of our individual existences are, but each line represents how I felt at that particular moment in time."

"But that's amazing. You should really try and get your work out to a large audience, people who will appreciate your story. It seems such a shame for everything to be stored away here, that art lovers aren't getting the chance to enjoy your sketches, a chance to read your lovely words."

He shrugged.

"That appears to be my fate."

"It doesn't have to be," she said with genuine feeling, as if his pictures had really stirred her emotions. "I know a few people, well, I say a few people, when I mean my Uncle Ronald. He's got his own gallery in the city, he's got loads of contacts. In fact, he's worked with the award-winning, multi-millionaire artist Rhea Hilton before."

"Really?" said Jacob, but with not quite the same degree of surprise as he may have done in the past. Chance, coincidence had, after all, played such a huge part in his life so far.

"Yes. And I'm sure if I took some samples to show him, he'd be blown away. Would you be happy for me to do that, to take a dozen or so sketches home with me?"

Jacob replied without hesitation. "Please do. Take what you want. Now I feel I understand what they really mean, I'm happy to show them to anyone who's interested."

Three days passed.

On the morning he expected another visit from Yvonne, Jacob managed to work for a welcome and prolonged period of time, completing what would be his final poem to accompany the Gradual Epiphany sketch that Yvonne had seen when she last called around.

Lost in a Dying Room
quiet room, empty room,
living room, dying room,
so many stillborn hours,
trapped in love-lost's barren womb.

And it was just as Jacob had carefully printed the last word that he felt a sharp, stabbing sensation to his chest. Gasping, he shot to his feet, only to stumble and fall, crashing to the floor in a fit of convulsions, a violent seizure that he would never recover from.

***

"Wait until you see all of this, Uncle Ronnie," said Yvonne, skipping around a sizeable puddle. "You're not going to believe it. The man's a genius. And the sheer volume of work he's done over the years is nothing short of spectac-ular. It's like he's devoted his entire life to one single idea."

"Well," said her uncle, sidestepping the same puddle, "if what you've shown me already is anything to go by, we could be about to make the artistic discovery of the century. I mean, my London contacts are all over me. He's like the new Robert Crumb or Ralph Steadman. I could probably get Mr Fallada exhibition after exhibition, and a small for-tune in commissions and advance sales to boot."

They knocked on the caravan door and waited. But there was no reply.

"Oh, that's odd," said Yvonne. "I wonder if he's having a nap. I'll just try the door."

She reached for the handle and turned. It opened, and she poked her head inside the caravan.

"Shit!" she said, when seeing Jacob Fallada sprawled out on the floor.

Rushing inside, she crouched beside him and felt for the pulse in his neck. It was unnecessary; his skin was so cold she could tell he had been dead for a considerable amount of time.

"Is he…is he dead?" asked her uncle as he clambered into the cramped, gloomy space.

"I'm afraid so," she replied, on her knees now, looking down at Jacob's painfully thin, wasted body, a man of only thirty-five who looked closer to seventy.

"Oh, I am sorry, dear. Life really is full of the cruellest ironies, is it not?"

She looked across at him.

"How do you mean?"

"That Mr Fallada may well have been but a handful of days from his big breakthrough, the moment he'd no doubt been waiting for all his life, only to…to die before he could enjoy his success."

Yvonne nodded solemnly and got to her feet.

"It's so sad," she said, wiping a tear from her eye. "He was such a nice man." She took a deep intake of breath and slowly exhaled. "And I guess we should make a few phone calls now, report the death to the appropriate authorities and all that. But we'll have to go to the end of the lane. You can't get a signal here."

"Yes, understood."

As he politely waited for his niece to pass through the door first, he caught sight of a picture on the dining-table.

"Wait, look at this," he said, picking up a beautifully rendered charcoal sketch of a straggly haired, hunched-over figure, undoubtedly a self-portrait of Jacob in the weeks before he died. Beneath this pitiful image were a few lines of verse entitled Other People.

Sometimes,
Robinson Crusoe
Doesn't seem like
Such a tragic character...

Lightning Source UK Ltd.
Milton Keynes UK
UKHW041625140819
347911UK00004B/234/P

9 781733 938815